HEAD OF THE CORNER

by the same author

ACROSS THE WATER
LAST DANCE WITH YOU

HEAD OF · THE CORNER

Grace Ingoldby

MICHAEL JOSEPH

London

To Edward

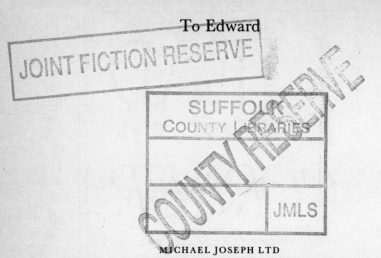

MICHAEL JOSEPH LTD

Published by the Penguin Group
27 Wrights Lane, London w8 5tz, England
Viking Penguin Inc., 40 West 23rd Street, New York, New York 10010, USA
Penguin Books Australia Ltd, Ringwood, Victoria, Australia
Penguin Books Canada Ltd, 2801 John Street, Markham, Ontario, Canada l3r 1b4
Penguin Books (NZ) Ltd, 182–190 Wairau Road, Auckland 10, New Zealand

Penguin Books Ltd, Registered Offices: Harmondsworth, Middlesex, England

First published in Great Britain 1988

Made and printed in Great Britain by
Richard Clay Ltd, Bungay, Suffolk
Filmset in Monophoto Baskerville

British Library Cataloguing in Publication Data

Ingoldby, Grace
Head of the corner.
I. Title
823'.914 [F]   PR6059.N52/

ISBN 0-7181-2980-6

Prologue

I am the light that will make safe the path, I am the door. I am the hammock slung for you between the silver birch trees. The sun is out and birds are singing, bees buzz; each little green leaf exquisitely made to dapple the book you're reading.

I love you.

As much as your mother did.

Should you fall on your back in some remote, inaccessible, barbed-wire corner of my universe I'll leave the others on the instant and come and seek you out. I'll carry you in my arms – how does that sound? Or round my neck, all gentleness, back to the comfort of the flock. I can't rest easy if you are out of my sight, you are that important to me.

I am the light and the love that never fails: omnipotent, omniscient and caring. You're panting on your back and the razor-ribbon wire cuts and stings like

I

blazes; just say you hear, or think you hear, the howl of a hungry wolf? Just say your nostrils quiver and your heart begins to pound with the sniff of it? Intuitively I know just where you are. It may seem dark to you between the beats of the beams of the lighthouse, and the sea is no postcard when you're disabled like this on the edge of a subsiding cliff and a long fall down; but you are special to me and I am your saviour, hold fast.

The sea's so deep, it rolls beneath you with a mighty suck. You imagine rocks and boulders, many-faceted, lacerating, rat-life in the gullies impenetrably black. The earth beneath your panting back groans and shifts, and doom between the lighthouse beats and darkness. I am the light, I'm coming.

No one has ever been, or will ever be, abandoned. Ask for grace and it will be forthcoming. The one who brought the plagues on the Egyptians will not desert you. But, and however, I am an old hand at the job, omnipotence palls me, and, to add that little sparkle to my light, I move in mysterious ways.

I

After a brief moment of glory in 660-something when St Feichin of Ballisodare, Sligo and from the stock of Con of a Hundred Battles lived as an anchorite in peace and humility on the island of Inishcara, its light has dimmed. The sea has eaten into it, years of indifference have muted its song; Inishcara now is only an island among other islands more famous than itself.

The mail boats take passengers out to Inishboffin, the island of the White Cow; Achil has beach bungalows and golf courses and Grace O'Malley's castle; Aran has sweaters and Synge. These islands, like Inishgowla and Inishoo, are described as heavens, 'delectably ringed with foam'. Inishcara has its foams, its moments, but although the black curraghs fish throughout these waters, none will come too close, for Inishcara has the misfortune and the advantage of being perfectly accessible by land. It is an inshore island where

3

at every tide the sea retreats to leave a wide and level expanse of sand over which, one imagines, St Feichin must have crossed dry shod.

Roughly oval, undistinguished; the holiness of Inishcara has evaporated leaving a barely tangible stillness in the air. Death is marked by a straggling graveyard, unfenced in a paradise of small and delicate wild flowers; emigration by its rank of broken houses now filled with farmers' straw. Light has dimmed but life still flickers from its one occupied building, which houses the five elderly sisters of St Dymphna. A convent past the prime of life, its almost empty rooms look out across the Atlantic to America and are mentioned briefly in the Bord Failte leaflet on North-west Connemara as a place for retreatants and holidaymakers where hospitality, *failte*, can be found.

Joe Reihill provisions the convent, his bar and grocery a repository of unfortunate and unimaginative bulk-buys. Value for money is an obsession with Joe; temptation in packets of ten times twenty, boxes and crates now stacked against him, dubious bargains that have turned him into a hoarder. His stock-room, locked and padlocked, is crammed with twenty-four-hour digital clocks, cocktail glasses, condiment sets, garden tools, calendars and spice jars, free gifts not displayed as they might have been – his customers have to ask. A middle-aged man with the growing sense in the past few years that he is marking, if not 'doing' time, he is prone to short, sharp rages and depressions which are somewhat more prolonged. His wife, who suffers from something glandular, is no help. Since their marriage twenty-seven years before she has grown in size but dwindled in authority, a curtain twitcher, a plaintive voice from a rather smelly downstairs room. Of their children only the younger remains at home;

4

Eileen 'does' for the convent and though only in her early twenties it looks quite possible that she may not find a mate.

It has been another bad year for the farmers who hug their pessimism like a destiny. The hay they won in June, squeezed into small heaps and covered with cloths held down by baling twine and stones, presently lies rotting in the fields. Hobbled donkeys haw haw, dogs bark and bite in the carcases of abandoned cars, and Germans, dressed to kill, fish happily in the rain. Long-tailed sheep stray along the little roads that wind down from the mountains from Letterfrack and beyond; less suicidal than usual they cling and lean away from the wet and wind into the prickle of the hedge.

Monsieur le Directeur, a power in the land and priest in charge of St Dymphna's convent, wakes up feeling seedy, remembers gratefully that the tide means he will not this morning have to say an early mass. Sleep is sanctuary: in his dreams he is in his native Belgium, just a boy wandering along the banks of the canal. In his practised hand the stones are accurate and satisfying; oblivious of passing time he pelts the bloated body of a drifting, drowned, brown dog.

Over on Inishcara Eileen chatters whilst waiting for the toast. She has trouble with her feet, one foot a half-size bigger than the other, now uncomfortably stuffed into a pair of new small shoes. Sister Euphrasia, a neat foot if ever there was one, commiserates in Belgian-English with Connemara lilt, awkward phrases often difficult to catch.

It is 7.14 a.m. by one of Reihill's digital clocks presented to the convent with some ceremony just last year. Richard Crosswhaite, professional retreatant, waits for toast, after which he will swallow a small

5

white pill. If the rain keeps off he will go to the garden, if it doesn't he will read; he is insulated and whatever the weather decides to do, he'll win. Min – white pills, blue pills, black and yellow wasp pills – breakfasts all alone. Less retreatant than recluse, she lies awake in a bed which has just been expertly, if a little roughly, tucked in and sorted out by Rachel, a young and saintly Australian, a nice bit of leg visible through her wrap-round Indian skirt, a goodly girl who likes to help others 'less fortunate' than herself. Nona Upton, hardy perennial, has been to the bathroom and is about to dress; it is the first day of her annual holiday and it feels glorious to be back.

II

The morning is new and cold, colder than England, damp. Visibility is poor today and the convent, closed in on itself in the centre of the island, sits it out beneath a sky of tailor's grey. The porteress's lodge is chilly and both the table and the chair are faintly sticky to the touch. The sash window is smudged with salt and a dribble of old rain lies along the sill; Nona is talking to her daughter Julia in her head.

'Of course it's cold, dear – it's not the Costa Brava. I don't go to Ireland for the sun.'

'Why do you go then?'

Nona ignores this and replaces the fire in the wall cupboard where it belongs. Sister Basil, the Reverend Mother, had needed it perhaps. She was older than Nona, although with nuns it is hard to be precise: Sister Agnes's age was common knowledge (easy when you're over eighty), Sister Euphrasia, Sister Basil and Sister

7

Godeleive were sixty-something and Sister Ignatius Antony was young. Nona stuck at fifty-something and she wasn't cold: she was warm that morning both inside and out.

Here she was, sitting as she had sat at the beginning of so many Augusts, a pile of blank white postcards in front of her, arranging what she might say. Her heart lifted as she touched the elastic band which clasped the cards – Inishcara. It was like that moment when Scarlett O'Hara pulled the carrot. Tara!

'Honestly mother.'

Tara was condemned. Julia's opinion of chill and rain in the summer, of Ireland in general and convents in particular, of the sort of Freudian whatever-it-was that explained her mother's refusal to use the fire, added up to something nasty.

'Suffering? For what, mother?'

Tara and the porteress's lodge. Nona's room, Nona's workroom for the duration. Spartan perhaps, definitely on the drab side, but welcome was the definition of its job. Nona's job as occupant of this room was to welcome here all visitors, loved and treated with love in the name of the Lord. The inescapable fact that most visitors were unappealing if not unlovable was irrelevant – a point neatly underlined by the room's sole decoration, a print, *Abraham Welcoming the Three Strangers by the Oaks at Mamre*, which bore the legend, 'I was a stranger and you took me in'.

She had already looked through the visitors book, also damp; she always did that before she launched herself on her PCs. How reassuring it was to see your own writing in such a book: a token, should you need one, that you really did exist. Nona's writing August after August; Sister Basil's writing – this had deteriorated, but then, really, it never had been

8

copperplate:

'Revd. Mère Génerale accompagnée de sa secretaire Soeur Bénigna.'

And this must be Rachel's writing for June and July and that explained the fire. Nona scrutinised the entries through spectacles which hung permanently on a gilt chain round her neck, conceding with some reluctance that the writing was, for an Australian and one so young, surprisingly well formed.

'Thank you so much, Rachel dear. I'll take over now.'

One had only to flick back to May – difficult to flick damp pages – that year of our Lord 1985, to see where Nona herself, on a flying visit, just a week, had signed Rachel Dixon in.

'How good of you, Rachel. The least I can do is take the August horror off your hands.'

A quiet year; the weather had been unusually unkind. Hardly anyone at all in June, apart from the Reverend Mother Génerale and Soeur Bénigna, a straggle of day trippers coinciding with the start of the school holidays; and outside now rain again and the tide quite wrong for crossing any morning of that week. Nona was not disappointed; on the contrary, she was pleased.

'I was a stranger and you took me in.' Let's face it, the quality of strangers had gone off.

'Welcome isn't cheap, Julia, *failte* costs.' That ghastly Muriel woman with the kidney stone; if Nona had her way she would have been a sight more selective, call it protective, but as a guest herself she could hardly interfere. No. Hospitality arrangements could not be altered: welcome was an inherited penance for the Sisters of St Dymphna, like periods, simply a fact of life.

9

'And part of the penance of community, Julia, is community itself. A martyrdom of pinpricks.'

'Mother!'

She was damned if she'd explain. Explain how nice it was occasionally, well, regularly, to go somewhere where you felt that you belonged. Somewhere where you felt on top as she did now. The nuns depended on her; surely Julia could see that? And there were other things that went quite deep. The same bed every year, the view from her window, Richard, the island, conversation, cards, companionship.

Julia had an enquiring mind. Nona had never established whether it was admiration or irritation which prompted this comment so frequently on her daughter's school reports. Julia asked a lot of questions but not, Nona suspected, because she was particularly eager for replies. Questions provided Julia with an opportunity to do what she thought she did best: tell people things in plain language, let them have it from the hip; tell them things about themselves that she had perceived and decided, quite ruthlessly, that they ought to know. Her timing was often excellent, like scenes from those afternoon radio plays when a deluded character is unpleasantly shown the light.

Where light was concerned, Nona hugged the gloom. Julia continued to ask her mother for Christmas, for holidays, but Nona wouldn't budge. Julia's husband was a sporting caver and speleologist, the grandchildren, Lawrence, Oliver and Drucie – all crampons and computers and contemptuous remarks about Arthur Ransome.

She imagined her daughter now in that busy London kitchen:

'Mother's gone off again. That place.'

Really, she must get on with it. Rachel's writing. She should never have confided in Rachel, in an Australian, that the hospitality side of convent life sometimes proved a bit too much.

'Don't let people get up your nose, Nona,' the girl had said.

Fate had placed the convent just west of the scenic loop and for that Nona heartily gave thanks. The convent was not well serviced: no souvenir shop and, apart from Eileen's fitful efforts at mealtimes, refreshment facilities nil. Americans, the sort who bought shelayleys and memoirs of Brendan Behan, sated themselves on tapestry bookmarks, holy pictures and hideously painted stones, were not keen. Only the intrepid hung around on the mainland until it was possible to cross the strand and when they got to Nona they were usually disappointed and disillusioned, if not visibly distressed. No cheap lobsters, no red petticoats, no shark-oil lamps, no fulmar-in-a-basket, no hint of a ceilidhe or a jig. In an average year, and it had been some time since they'd had one, visitors to Iniscara divided somewhat ironically into two diametrically opposed camps: serious environmentalists, Scandinavians, Germans, reliable cars parked cautiously on the opposite shore, and the sort of old hippies, 'blow-ins' the Irish called them, who wilfully destroyed the very fauna and flora in which the former party gutturally rejoiced.

Nona had tackled the nuns on this one. Told them quite directly that their famous hospitality was being used.

'That's what it's there for,' Sister Basil had said.

III

Quiet and still, only the convent and the sheep.

Visibility has improved and the island, cut off this morning by the sea, reveals itself to be ringed not only with 'delectable foams' but also with parts of rusted cars, obsolete domestic machinery and old boots.

Min, propped up in bed but still unable to see anything but sky from her window, knows that Nona has arrived, is in the lodge, is writing postcards, that all is well, 'as well as can be expected'. All alone she fights the resignation that is beginning, she knows it, to set in.

Min has lived with the sisters of St Dymphna for seventeen years. It wasn't meant to be so long; it didn't begin like that and it is only now that she has looked at it, wondered at the time she's spent, only now that she thinks of it because she knows it is about to end.

Nona has, has always had, choices that Min somehow had to do without. Even this morning Nona could get up and look through the window of the porteress's lodge. Nona could see what Min sees only in her mind's eye: the band of small fields hopelessly edged by fallen stones, the grey boulders, the bog holes, the tufts of wool clinging on the barbed wire that keeps the sheep out of the houses which will be their larders when there is no more grass to find. Nona couldn't quite see the sand road that leads past the houses and to the convent, but the line of it, marked by the telephone poles darkened by the rain and the wires that loop and sag, the line of it would be clear. She could see what Min is fixed on: the graveyard at the very edge of the island, its headstones looking out at the mainland across the covered strand. The stones reeling at all angles, the graveyard sloping, slipping into the sea, the stones which watch what's going on but which, like Min, cannot intervene. Eileen going back across to her father, helping her cousin Sylvester to unload the Harp lorry or to stack the empties out the back. Off with Sylvester in the estate car, a trip to the cash and carry and then ... Monsieur le Directeur's grey Wolsey and Jim appearing from behind a hedge and nipping into Reihill's for a quick one when the Wolsey has turned off. The Dorises round at the O'Rileys' because their children are off school. The little ones running cars into puddles and the dogs barking after the Wolsey, racing each other and biting at the tyres.

The headstones, taking note of passing life, watching.

Twenty-four days ago, and she's not letting anything slide now, she's counting every day, Rachel and Sister Ignatius Antony moved her down and out of the chambrette – seventeen years – and into this new room. In the grand old days of fifty years ago this was the postulants'

13

parlour; Belgian, Irish, English and American aspirants sat here. 'More in the centre of things,' they told her, 'just off the big corridor, the trunk road.' Just off it, but it may as well be the band of fields or the leaning standing stones. The big corridor, the trunk road, and Min, nicely thank you, in a cul-de-sac just off.

She tests them and – out of delicacy? –they lie.

'I'm in the lay-by.'

'Only a pit stop, Min.'

'Jim is coming to mend your windows before the winter comes' – this too is a sort of trick.

'I can't see out of the window and I won't be here in the winter.'

'A fierce draught,' they say, but why do they want to mend her window when the house is already full of wind? The weather comes from all directions, it's wrecking Richard's attempt at a garden; seventeen years – if he had come to her she could have told him that here the weather always wins. On her own she hears the wind get in, race down the corridor, ruffling the niches of the saints in the architraves in the wall, the saints with their silk flowers, the very same flowers they twist into wreaths and place beside the stones.

The lay-out of the convent she knows so well reveals its priorities: the big corridor, the trunk road, leads directly to the chapel and to God. The porteress's lodge is as distant from the chapel as it can be: *failte* certainly, but only at arm's length. Spiritual life is easier to lead than a secular one: earthly food carried from the kitchen to the retreatants' refectory, brought down here to her on the trolley, skin formed on the custard, white sauce, gravy, luke warm if not cold. Spiritual life is ordered but it cannot catch the wind; the wind is pagan and this thought gives Min joy. The door to the chapel, though metaphorically always at least ajar, is closed against it.

Min listens as the wind tears down the corridor, meets the door, is miffed of satisfaction and roars back.

'I can hear the wind but it isn't in my room. Why is Jim coming to mend my window?'

Min has taken to swearing into her pillow and does so now. She's going to think of every obscenity she can remember and when she gets stuck she'll invent.

'You've no idea, Min, but then how could you have? You always led such a pleasant sheltered life.'

They'll think it's tears, the wet on her pillow, but knowing it's spit and dribble and venom, Min, in the lay-by, holds fast. 'A nice spot for a picnic. Off the beaten track', plenty of sound effects and a fifteen-inch view of the sky.

IV

Like the Greeks, the sisters of St Dymphna considered a readiness to offer hospitality a criterion which distinguished civilised people from barbarians. Welcome was written on the mat.

The tradition of hospitality, the penance, went right back and, as usual in Ireland, history was all. The daughter of a heathen Irish prince had fled from her incestuous widowed father with her chaplain Gerebernus. They were caught and both slain and the name 'Dymphna' had been found on a brick with the coffins. Since then the Order of St Dymphna, the Order of the Brick, had become famous for its intercession. By the end of the thirteenth century St Dymphna was widely regarded as the patroness of travellers and the insane. This convent had a sister house in Belgium; a feature of it, considered to be remarkably enlightened then and now, was its tradition of hospitality plus its system of boarding out suitable patients and travellers in private houses throughout the neighbourhood and integrating them into normal society. The problem on and around Inishcara was the lack of normal society, the lack of 'society' to speak of at all; the convent could do no better than to tackle whatever turned up on its doorstep at source.

In this event the porteress doubled as chaperone, showed visitors which part of the chapel they could use, which areas of the garden were available for them to take photographs of each other and, if visible, the view. Snaps of the nuns were not encouraged and hard to acquire in any instance as the sisters spent most of their day coralled, isolated from the action, in places known as 'Sisters' Private Parts'. A tourist encroaching on these sanctuaries was likely to be treated in the same manner as a straying sheep; a waving of black-sleeved arms and the Belgian equivalent of something mild like 'shoo'. Of all the sisters only Sister Agnes was fierce; she had not got past eighty without a struggle, she did not like to be disturbed and she was known to have used her pincushion as a missile and occasionally resorted to small stones.

Such incidents, reprimanded by the Reverend Mother, were much talked about and giggled over by the sisters, but apart from these rare occurrences, the sighting of a stranger as disorientating as news of walking on the moon, the nuns lived a quiet life, moving freely and comfortably in a routine that was as reassuring, if not as sloppy, as Eileen's oldest pair of shoes.

A martyrdom of pinpricks, visitors were a distraction from the daily game of insert-the-catheter, the sisters probing and poking beneath each other's skins. The penance of community, community itself, the thorn not blunted by familiarity or time. Trifling idiosyncracies loomed large in their communal life, throwing long shadows across their quest to reach the light. Sister Ignatius Antony was a fresh-air freak, Sister Euphrasia hugged a fug. To mortify herself Sister Antony closed windows opened, for the same reason, by Sister Euphrasia. Friction between them was never given voice; who opened and who closed windows became ever more complicated and time only served to tangle the ball of mixed-up motives which rolled between the two of them each day. Celibate they might be but, experienced warriors in a battle of attrition, they knew more about the married state than most.

Only in one relationship did this potentially pyrotechnic party of women come together as a group and this was in their unstinting devotion to Monsieur le Directeur, an uninspiring and pasty-faced Belgian whom they worshipped with a zeal impossible to comprehend. The retreatants at the convent used him when they wanted him: like a swimming pool or a tennis court he was a facility, albeit rather poorly kept up. Nona had no time for him at all, Eileen remarked on his appetite, Min found something menacing about his gloves. The sisters loved him; his position as head of their small family was secure.

That this small world must be preserved Nona had never once had any doubt. What she intended to protect by her somewhat restrained welcome in the porteress's lodge was what the nuns had almost incidentally created by themselves, this haven of quiet and calm.

'A haven of quiet and calm'; she wrote it on one of her cards.

As per, Nona had arrived at Inishcara absolutely whacked. She sat back for a moment and took two

Polos from the tube in her handbag. Looking at her watch she fondly imagined Eileen up to her usual tricks; the coffee was very late. She had another Polo and another; the journey had always been a nightmare but even on a rough sea – 'Weather ghastly' – the leaving of London, of work and particularly of Julia never failed to do the trick. To relax her. She felt the stress climb as she considered the word 'relax'. Relax and I'll tread on your face.

'Already so refreshed.'

Tired yes, but the anticipated pleasure of seeing everyone again; those long afternoons they spent playing cards. Racing Demon was Richard's favourite – he got excited, laughing and shouting, fairly chucking the cards across the table.

She hadn't seen anyone yet except for Min – she popped in on Min, such a sweet little room and so in the centre of things – she hadn't seen anyone that morning – work came first. She'd been straight to Sister Basil and offered her services – as she joked, 'checked in'. Eileen would surely bring the coffee in a minute and she'd have her cards done well before lunch. She had a present for Eileen, make-up, and one for Richard, Rachel, Min – presents for everyone in the tray on top of her case. And she wanted to iron one or two things.

'Dressing like a gypsy.'

She liked to keep up appearances: as porteress she felt obliged to look a little smart. It was quite a struggle looking good but no one need know that. Just how much Nona earned from 'my silly little jobs', was a well-kept secret even from Julia who, of course, had asked. Julia insisted that 'at bottom' (she had a big one) everything was economic, wars, relationships, the lot, and what you were paid amounted to a ranking of respect. Her husband, sporting caver, computer consultant, didn't get out of bed for less than £100. Nona ate a Polo to forget.

The lizard handbag which she now closed to arrest the Polo flow was mended in several places and smelt of 'Dab-it-off' inside. If you studied it closely the marks of a leaking biro were still visible on the kid – dear, she had been so cross with herself over that! She touched her hair with a nervous gesture; did it suit her quite so short? She wore it shorter these last years than she had done, on her hairdresser's advice. Twice a year she had it permed professionally and had become quite expert at keeping it up by home-perming in between times at her flat. She had in fact done this several weeks before she came over. Julia, who might have helped her to do it if they had been closer, failed to tell her about the piece that had escaped her at the back.

Now she smoothed the silk scarf round her throat; she touched herself a lot – touch, people do that when they live alone. 'We can't all be princesses, Eileen, but we can have a touch of luxury round the neck.' Min's present was a little scarf Drucie had given to Nona for her birthday but it wasn't quite her blue, rather a hard blue actually. Was it mean to give Min something that she herself didn't like? No, it wasn't: the one thing you mustn't do is change your attitude towards people simply because they're ill.

She looked at the door as if coffee might come through it and then up at Abraham on the wall.

'Dear Andrew,' she would write to the new, young, producer at the BBC, 'I have only to wave goodbye to London and my head is teeming with exciting new ideas.' Or, 'Andrew – one or two ideas already that I think might interest you.' Cruelty to contributors. In six parts?

What a nightmare it all was, she frequently confided in Min – Min was so interested in Nona Upton's life – 'So sadly addicted to fashion you know, current trends'. It was people like Nona who had to jog their memories now and then, remind them, gently, of what was what. Remind them of people, 'like you Min', ill in bed in a world that wasn't London, people who wanted to listen to something uncontentious, nice.

'You are lucky, Nona.'

'You make your own luck, Min.'

And it added up to what Julia called a 'knack', Nona a technique.

'You have to make it sound as if you're talking to one person, Min, not addressing the Third World from a plinth.'

You had to make it intimate, make it all seem easy, act it into the mike. You had to be a bit of a performer and she was certainly that, like the way she had to pretend that she wasn't offended, hadn't been hurt. Hadn't noticed the slight, was accustomed to going unrecognised, to being kept waiting, even though she'd been in and out of those imposing London buildings for years and years and years.

This particular producer, whose postcard remained so blank, was the proud owner of a new slot. 'Dear Andrew' – she was even a bit anxious about that – 'Dear Andrew, I have witnessed the genesis, life and death of more new slots . . .'

'The young are so impatient, Min, so keen to make their mark; think of themselves more than the audience, only interested in something that gets them three columns of criticism in the press.' And what was worse was the way they upped and left, moved on, just as one had established some sort of rapport. 'Fun, yes, Min, but the sort of fun that takes a high emotional toll.'

The nuns were awfully sweet. They listened to all her programmes when they could; they were always so courteous, so kind, keeping cuttings for her, remembering in detail. Sister Basil said she really didn't know how on earth Nona came up with so many bright ideas! It was nice to know they were listening, far away from Bush House, gathered round the radio in their own Salle de Fête. Sometimes, when she babysat for Julia she let one or other of the grandchildren stay up: 'Hear Granny's voice coming out of the radio'. They couldn't concentrate for long – well they were far too young – but something Lawrence had said last time when they were listening stayed with her.

'Will you go on giving talks, Granny, when you've nothing left to say?'

She must do this postcard for Andrew, show she was on the ball.

'I've had something on my mind for some time that I'd like your advice about,' she wrote; she pandered, giant panda – it was the only acceptable approach.

'You see, Min dear, you have to make them feel they're something even though you know that they are not. They must sense that you consider them to be important arbiters of taste.'

Taste – if only she'd got into food.

'That's the area now, Min – food is no longer simply something that you eat.'

Food and general health. In May Rachel Dixon had let slip – well, she never stopped talking about herself – that she had been anorexic. Taking a pad from her bag she now wrote, 'Talk to R. about A.' and then, 'Min must have more than eggs, something nourishing, light. Bengers? Complan? and treats if at all poss. Lemon tea? Champagne?'

'Glorious as ever,' she wrote to Julia. 'Let me know if there's anything you want for the children.'

She wouldn't let her know, 'Honestly Mother they prefer money', nor could Nona knit anything because her grandchildren, Lawrence especially, loathed wool. She questioned Lawrence about this when they were on their own to see what he really felt and it was obvious that his love of acrylic went deep: 'I only wear sweatshirts,' he insisted, 'things that go into Mummy's machine.'

'Don't touch it, mother. I'll do it.'

What did she think that mother was used to: a washboard, a fast-running river and a stone?

'Catching up on all the gossip, tell you all.'

A cup of coffee at this stage of the morning begged an element of surprise.

'Youth culture's as dead as a Dodo, Andrew. Don't you know?'

And just relax. Relax. All this is familiar to you, Nona Upton: Eileen has forgotten to bring the coffee again and it's raining and it takes a day or so to get acclimatised and to put aside all worries about work. She finished the cards, clicked the pen, closed the lizard bag. Nothing's new, nothing's changed, it's the same old me but I'm home now, people to see, presents to give, cards to play ... She stroked her face absent-mindedly; even Sister Ignatius Antony looked a bit crêpey this year – that ghastly habit of not moisturising their necks. Gently she stroked her skin, removed her glasses from her nose and let them swing.

V

Min, before the pearly gates you must explain. Explain
how even butterflies get sick of things; how, fed up with
flying, they stray into cupboards and get hooked. Some
change in the atmosphere affects them and landing on
the earth the world looks different: the minutiae of it
attract them, pulls them in. Brillo pads and scourers,
Ajax, Vim and Frish, stoppered plastic one may squirt
through, nozzles one may aim, become as pleasing to the
antennae and quite as necessary as the perfumery coun-
ters, the haberdashery departments where they once
fluttered to a halt. The scullery becomes for them what
the buddleia once was, mimicking the pussmoths; those
dull cousins' eyes tightly closed, clinging into corners of
dusty panes of glass, the butterflies settle and stop. They
fold their wings up, like a penknife, like an envelope, and
consider themselves disguised.

Min did it, seventeen years ago; Min did it, which

proves it can be done. She made herself invisible, horrible – her fault. Now too late to tango, she saw herself as they'd seen her: her retreating figure, always retreating, heading down the trunk road with a brush. Clever camouflage, part of the landscape, overall up to the neck and, should the convent have caught fire, or suddenly subsided into the sea, a list of names in a bureau drawer would remind them of her and her name would be placed on the roll of missing and feared dead.

Well done Min.

In the tiny sphere of St Dymphna's convent where those taken in paradoxically spent much of their time anxiously looking out, Min had been more practical than most. Her name appeared in the visitors book in December 1967, Christmas *failte*; she was forty-four, and in her handbag then and now she keeps a photograph of herself at the age of eight, taken on a beach more splendid than any round these shores. The breasts are flat and the hair is straight, the pose is unremarkable but the eyes have it, levelled at the camera, brown and round, marked in the face as stubborn little stones.

Min liked the convent *circa* '67; she liked it very much. The nuns' unquestioning, altogether non-judgemental behaviour, which annoyed other visitors so much that they would run after the sisters volunteering information and at one and the same time always feeling faintly dissatisfied and ignored, seemed to her just the very thing. It had been a rush to reach the convent, an impulse, and she'd done it in a fog. When the fog cleared a little, when she got back some of her breath, she wrote a letter to her husband full of information but quite without excuse. Robert was her husband's name and she wrote to Robert suggesting –

quite something in those days – whatever he wanted, separation or divorce. Other separated men lost their houses and their children and had their belongings cut in half; some even lost their cars. He had lost only a wife; only pride and habit had been dented and the panel could be simply beaten out. She wanted nothing from him except to be left alone; brutally insulted, he let her stew.

At first she had imagined that there would be books she would want to read or painting to do, flowers to arrange, bonnets to trim, middle-class pursuits, but this legacy from the old world wouldn't fit. She had come to avoid Christmas 1967; 1968 rolled in. Sister Agnes, light on her feet in those days, still very much in her prime, suggested she might like to help.

Help. It caught her imagination, more than reading, more than sunset over the water or orchids in a jar: housework, previously meaningless, suddenly made good sense.

The utter calm after disaster, the calm of being occupied and seeing a result and the lack of anxiety, relief, when you knew that it would be undone and that you could, without explanation or excuse, do it all again. The tools of the trade were shown to her as the tools of life had never been. No one had ever sat Min on their knee and explained things to her in quite this way before. She had never been still long enough, only long enough to slip into the edge of that photo, other photos, wedding photos; now she was ready for it and it was there.

In another life she might have made a fine solicitor or a clerk, for it was the precedent of convent life, convent cleaning, that appealed to her the most. Here were the cupboards, utterly regulated, already established and, would you believe it, cleaned once a month

26

themselves! And when you cleaned the cupboards you put the contents back in the same order so that, unlike life, you opened a cupboard and found everything where you expected it would be. The routine and the ritual, the motion of it and the size of the convent which gave it point; thinking about dust and anticipating it, and cobwebs, fingermarks, tarnish, spills; she had thought she might become absorbed in another sort of brushwork but this was far, far better than anything like that. Talent did not apply, thoroughness did; the mysteries of that shine, that colour, that corner, could all quite simply be explained.

Cleaning cut you off from other people like a screen; cleaning gave you purpose, was its own excuse. Cleaning wouldn't frighten you by ending, cleaning wouldn't stop and in a convent where perfection was pursued there was always, would always be, something else to do. Thrift prolonged it, lovely thrift; the slither of old polish left in the tin, the turning for a clean piece of cloth, the cobble and the making-do. You had to think a little but not too much and it wasn't the sort of thinking, the circular sort, the tumbler, that made you hate yourself or what you had become, not the sort of thinking Min had grown to dread. *Circa* '67, '68; and in the beginning Min had not used any money, neither answered the door nor the telephone, nor received or written any mail.

'Bar the door of thy senses and dwell therein guarding thy heart against all images and shapes of earthly things'; for the art of total preoccupation she turned to the tutelage of the nuns. She watched the sisters, listened to them, observed the way in which they all behaved. By the late sixties the days of flowing habits and winged veils had passed even there on Inishcara; the secret lay in imagining blinkers and

27

enclosure and it was not an easy thing to do. At the beginning, and the season made it easier, she had stayed as much as possible indoors, where no bird could sing to her or flower open up. She grew pale as a romantic heroine, she lost weight, she held on. The nuns were taught to keep their thoughts within the brackets of sunrise and sunset; Min kept hers in the cupboard. Love and music were out right at the beginning and the sort of feeling deep inside when you let yourself imagine just a fragment of a scene, meeting at the station, someone coming home. There was a knack to living which she had never mastered but the confined life of a convent seemed to offer her a chance. With help you too could grow out of the detail of your past. It had to do with eyes forward and no looking back; what Sister Agnes called, 'custody of the eyes'. You thought of Wednesday and Thursday, the weekend, but not which weekend or which Thursday or how many weekends or Thursdays you had spent like this. It was about living day to day, floor to floor, statue to statue, dust to dust, cupboard to sink and wringing out the cloth. One thought she couldn't shift she threaded with a piece of string and hung around her neck: the memory, or perhaps the fact, that not all the arms in the world, linked up and 'Auld Lang Syne', could protect you from its sorrows.

Cleanliness might be next to Godliness; it was certainly next to peace. Soon she was outside in the garden, soon she could look at the kittens round the kitchen door. Soon she was able to clean the madonna statue which the sisters called *The Bliss*. With a toothbrush she scooped out the blown sand which settled daily over its inscription: '*Cantate Domino Canticum Novum: Quia Mirabilia Fecit*' – 'Sing the Lord a new song, a song of wonder at his doing'; she never read a word. She wiped the statue and she brushed it with all the appropriate tools; she cleaned it and enjoyed cleaning it without acknowledging the folds in the garments, the figure of the woman, or the swaddled shape of the baby cradled in its arms.

How hopeless I was at the beginning, Min thought now, remembering those days when the stone bumped against her chest and her hands clutched desperately at the soggy cloth; how she had improved herself, how much she had lost.

Not a zombie but a drip, she thought, reflecting on how she'd willingly learnt the ropes. You must deceive yourself and in doing so you would deceive other people. The nuns called it retreat but she knew, always knew, it was escape. You learnt the discipline of knowing how much you could explore, how far you could go, how much you could think about, what you could look at and listen to without crumbling. How far you could progress in perfecting this everyday nothing, stretching it a little more each day like a ballet dancer mastering her body; hara-kiri the butterfly stuck with a pin.

VI

Convent life is heavily punctuated; Nona tripped on a comma during lunch. She was talking to Richard, she'd blushed, felt her face colour up and flush when she'd seen him.

'You've been coming here for six years, Richard. Terrible! And me for ten.'

'No one goes back as far as you do, Nona.'

Except Min.

'The elephant remembers the ancient trackways through the forest,' she replied, negotiating her way to a place at the table beside him. Richard always sat in the middle of the table: it was sensible to protect oneself from draughts.

Always in the same spot; typical of him – he loved everything that was old and solid and the same. She'd never seen his house but over the years he'd mentioned this and that about it. It was an old house apparently, it sounded heavenly; she was interested in the house, interested in everything he did. He was a collector – inkwells; he'd been quite sniffy about Monsieur le Directeur's collection of Limoges. He always came in August, regular as the clock – perhaps he'd retired or something, she didn't know – but lately he'd come in spring and prolonged his August visit into early autumn. He'd got quite wrapped up in the convent garden; he loved gardening. Spring and autumn were the times when gardens did things, weren't they, and that's why he came then. They'd just missed each other in May which was a pity, so it was a year since she had seen him and she'd blushed.

It was always a bit formal at the beginning but they were old friends, allies, and throughout the year she kept in touch. Not letters: something had stopped her from writing him letters, some instinct told her that letters were not what he would want. Snappy postcards were more the thing for him – cards from the National Portrait Gallery were her first choice. She remembered, the elephant, exactly which ones she'd already sent because it would be boring of her, disappointing for him, to send the same thing twice. Once and only once she had thought of phoning him; she'd just had her veins done and Julia suggested that she travelled across with him. She'd nearly phoned but instinct stopped her; Julia didn't know him, didn't know he wouldn't want to set a precedent like that.

This year she'd bought him such a lovely present; a book called *The Maze Maker*, a real find that combined all the things he loved. She was telling him about it when the comma tripped her up. She hadn't noticed Rachel leave her place at the table or move to the head of it.

Richard gestured to her, said, 'A bit of hush.'

Rachel was standing at a lectern – now where had that thing come from? Nona pulled a face at Richard which he didn't see. She had talked so much that her plate of food was still unfinished. In the silence she realised they were waiting for her; she put her knife and fork quickly to one side as Rachel cleared her throat.

'I've chosen this little reading for Nona because of the marvellous job she does as porteress and because we all welcome her here again in the name of Christ our Lord.'

Eileen crossed herself, Nona blushed again.

'It comes from the gospel of St Matthew:' – again the clearing of the throat, the voice of Australia – '"Take heed that ye do not your alms before men, to be seen of them: otherwise ye have no reward of your Father which is in heaven. Therefore when thou doest thine alms, do not sound a trumpet before thee, as the hypocrites do in the synagogues and in the streets, that they may have glory of men!"' She paused for breath, '"Verily I say unto you, They have their reward. But when thou doest alms, let not thy left hand know what thy right hand doeth"' – more breath and slowing down for the punch line – '"That thine alms may be in secret: and the Father which seeth in secret himself shall reward thee openly".'

'Well.'

'Hello Nona,' – Rachel had squeezed in beside Nona on the bench – 'you didn't mind that did you? Not embarrassed?'

'Not at all.'

'We started these little readings a couple of weeks ago – the idea came to me in bed!' Ha, ha. 'I don't know how you feel about it – you're quite free to choose something and do one yourself.'

32

'Thank you.'

'I really like Matthew, don't you? He has to be every-one's favourite, don't you think?'

Nona had noticed that Rachel had a missal in her hand, Richard was talking to Eileen, Rachel smelt of patchouli or something. She fiddled with the ribbon markers in her book.

'There's this brilliant bit in Corinthians: "Charity is patient, is kind: charity feels no envy, charity is never perverse."'

Richard wasn't really talking to Eileen but simply trying to get her to pass the pudding which being Wednesday was ice cream. Things sometimes stopped at Eileen, trays failed to move on. The faces at the table, Eileen, Rachel, Richard – she hadn't even thought about the missing Min.

'I saw Min yesterday.'

'Not this morning though,' the detective.

'No. I went straight to the lodge ("that thine alms may be in secret"). I thought I'd pop in after lunch. I was thinking, Rachel, perhaps there ought to be a rota including us and the sisters: it's so miserable to be ill.'

Rachel had turned to Richard. 'Fine.'

She was hardly listening to Nona.

'We could get visiting sorted out on a regular basis. If you're ill you do need time to sleep – you can't have people popping in all day long.'

'Right.' She wasn't interested.

'I'll organise something, shall I?' Nona said.

'Right.'

'Rather odd, wouldn't you say?' Nona questioned Richard as they took a turn in the wet garden after lunch, 'Religious readings during mealtimes . . .'

33

'Well, it is a religious house, Nona.'

Richard was being pompous. Nona didn't mind – she felt oblivious even if she had just been ticked off. She did a small middle-aged skip on the cinder path. The present was a hit: he was delighted with it. A joint present – his birthday was on 31 July. It struck her that he couldn't really have retired; by her reckoning he was only fifty-six.

'Perhaps you're getting religious in your old age,' she said to tease him. 'Now show me this marvellous maze.'

'Not a great deal happening now,' he began with his normal absorption. What a super present she'd given him. 'I'll have to dip into that book. How super of you, Nona, you are too good.'

She glowed, short and stubby and old, his elephant, his dog. 'Well,' she laughed as they walked down the damp slope, 'it did seem to have your name on it, you know.'

Together they studied the maze. He showed her proudly where he had done some 'in-filling' with new plants.

'I never thought those would take.' He pointed at small straggly bits, the cuttings. Nona sighed with pleasure.

It was a most unusual maze made of veronica and fuchsia, like a flag of red and blue. After the rain the veronica leaves had a beetle gloss; sometimes Nona saw veronica in England, dusty and silly and small, she would touch it, remember.

'It's lovely.'

'It's not much really.'

'Oh it is, it is.'

It was, and they looked at it for a long time. In her anxiety to go out with Richard, Nona had forgotten to

34

change her shoes – God knows what damage she'd done to the heels. The wind blew from the west and the air was damp and cold, Richard insulated by enthusiasm.

'I've got a surprise for you,' he said.

They turned away from the maze and the view of the sea back up the soggy cinder path and round towards the tiny paved area outside the Salle St Anne, the dry stone wall set against the wind with *The Bliss* set into it.

'*Cantate Domino . . .*' The stone madonna with the baby in her arms.

'Now just wait for this,' he said.

Years ago, sitting there with Richard catching a little evening sun, he had told her that *The Bliss* had the look of his old nanny. It was rather sweet, wasn't it? Just one of their secrets. Why should she hound him on the telephone or wish to write him letters when he freely gave her things like this?

'Now watch where you tread.'

Her shoes.

'We've made a little knot garden. I bet you didn't see that in the dark.'

She couldn't see much now.

'Elizabethan,' he said. She made a mental note. 'See? The little box hedges?'

Nona could just see them, two inches above the ground.

Richard stroked them with his palm. 'Perish the weather. The wind's the worst of it but they're just about sheltered here. They should be very good. I persuaded Jim to help me – he carted over sacks of Irish peat moss. At least the rain damps it so it doesn't blow away. Jim did the heavy work, moving out the stones. Look,' – he pointed to something trailing that

35

Nona didn't recognise – 'that's Rachel's: she's full of good ideas.'

A pile of paving stones had been removed to make the garden, a hexagon of muddy little spaces boxed in by this sparse and rather hairless hedge. Nona looked but found it difficult to think of anything appropriate to say. The labels were larger than the plants they were attached to; he squatted down beside them, read them out lovingly in Latin.

'The idea is that one walks over them. Not now, of course, not yet,' he added, noticing the movement of her foot. 'Like a camomile lawn, Nona, you know.'

She didn't know but looked as if she did. The notion of walking over plants seemed a little self-defeating. It was hard to imagine these weedy little green things springing up like heather. Rachel full of ideas; survival of the trailing plant obviously a matter of strong faith.

'Well,' she said.

'I thought you'd be interested.'

'I am.'

'An awful lot more work to do on it, of course.'

'Isn't there always?' she replied.

'The art of gardening is that of deferred gratification, my dear.' He was pompous again but this time she was irritated. 'Making something for posterity, a drop in the ocean . . .'

'Yes.'

'Seaweed's a good organic fertiliser but it takes such a devil of a time to break it down. This stuff's easier to handle and if Eileen could just remember to separate vegetable refuse from the rest of it and take it down to the compost bin . . .'

*

'You're freezing, Mother.'
   'I'm boiling.'
   'You're quite blue with cold.'

VII

You had to attune yourself to Inishcara; it took a bit of
time. Rather a dreary little knot, Nona thought, scrap-
ing the grass and cinders from her shoes. She had
listened to Richard until guilt made her beg leave to
visit Min. She'd seen her but not spoken to her. Min
had been asleep.

'A queer change in her,' Eileen said at lunchtime.
She didn't want a different Min.

Upstairs in her chambrette Nona straightened the
tissue on the hard blue scarf. She didn't want a different Min. The salt got in everywhere, the mirrors were
clouded by it. She repaired the damage to her hair,
applied her lipstick. Relax.

The chambrette calmed her. She always had the
same one; the view from its little window was as
familiar as the mouth she painted in the glass. Eileen
had been thrilled with the make-up, Min would love

the little scarf . . . England seemed so far away. In London she fed her memories of Inishcara with a series of mental pictures, imaginary photographs, still lifes: She and Richard at the card table; she and Richard by *The Bliss*, Nona and Sister Basil; Sister Ignatius Antony with her ankle in plaster, laughing like a horse. Min with a duster, Eileen feeding hens, handyman Jim up a ladder, Monsieur le Directeur huddled in his car. Sister Euphrasia, Sister Godeleive, Rachel Dixon – 'No more arbitrary than an orthodox family, Julia.' Because of the weather, real photographs always came out rather dark and postcards were ridiculous: glossy ponies, emerald greens, exaggerated blues. Her imaginary pictures were all framed and in London she took them out and looked at them with love. And this view was important to her, this view out of her little window. The nuns changed their chambrettes every year: it was part of their admirable self-denial. Nothing belonged to them; they held things in stewardship, 'for nuns getting attached to things is wrong'. The elephant was only human; she had her little window back again, she had her bed.

VIII

An odd summer for Min: no wasps. Rachel came to cut her fingernails; twenty-four days I cling on.

'We must cut your toenails, too.'

Must we?

After the nails Rachel said it would be lovely for her to have a long chat with Nona; Rachel decided, Min remembered . . .

When Robert had his accident. It was during the war and they had to borrow petrol to get to the cottage hospital, a bite-on-a-cork joint – everyone had stories about that place. There was a woman waiting with her. Even in the war they loved an accident; she went on and on about how awful the hospital was – once, she said, she'd seen an old man wheeled out into the corridor to die. Wheeled out! Min's bed had no wheels, she complained. Rachel thought she was rambling – they all did. Min considered the manner in which they misinterpreted, systematically misinterpreted what she said these days. Convenience? A Conspiracy? – She was in a lay-by, a passing-bay.

'Die here, it's easier for Eileen.'

Perhaps the nuns objected to the feet of strangers up their stairs, undertakers. Beeswax and turpentine on the banisters rubbed in and rubbed off, the corridor finished with the long handled broom with the wadded concrete pad. Yes, to die in the place you had lived in for years – but it all looked different on your back. She heard the rain but couldn't smell it, see it; at night the sweep of the lighthouse beam, the pictures on the ceiling.

Just off the trunk road, they all trooped in. The nuns came before the start of their long silence, making the sign of the cross. They expected a great deal of her now that she was ill; 'could try harder' – like parents, they were easily disappointed. She was expected to be enthusiastic, grateful and pleased, long-suffering, continent, religious and, being prone, to listen. They came and went; she picked over the sentences and phrases, expanded the argument, but they wanted her to listen, not to talk.

'You can't win with some people,' she teased them but they had no sense of humour.

'I'm not quite with you, Min dear.' They wouldn't take it up.

For form's sake they asked her what she wanted, for convenience they decided what she should have. A radio by the bed, a rota.

'She's very muddled.'

Nothing had ever been so clear.

Walled in like St Feichin, Min addressed the able-bodied through a fog. Whose fog? Their fog. Treat me like a human being, she suggested, or treat me like a dog. In England dogs are almost human beings; try and treat me like a dog. As frightened as a little child by the bloody calm, the acceptance that surrounded her; dog and God, not a muddle, clear. It looks like a whimper to you but it's a bang for me: the muffled sound of the fog horn in the sea mist, the bell from Feroonagh rock.

'Life goes on,' they said, leaving her; but so does mine, you idiots, so does mine!

Alone she sent up flares into the darkness, everything, anything: I cleaned the corridor, I washed the cloth, I murdered my husband, I owe money, there's opium under my bed. The only thing they responded to was 'I want to go to the lavatory'; how could she want to go when she had eaten and drunk so little?

'She thinks she wants to go but she doesn't really.'

Oh God.

What the dickens did she need a scarf for? She looked at it like an actress, half looked at it, languid, listless; she didn't say thank you for it either, she gave it a look of reproach.

'You're tired.'

'I'm isolated.'

'You're upset because you're tired.'

'You can't win with some people.'

And after that she closed her eyes and sulked. Eyes closed, she willed Nona to go away, she willed and willed. Just a glance had shown that Nona looked more tired than Min felt. Nona was saying something about Richard, Rachel and a rota . . . Why have I no choice? I can't pick the chocolates that I want. I can't go down another layer. I can't choose, I can't choose, I'm not consulted. I'm pestered like a baby, chucked under the chin, pestered like a baby in a pram. Poke your nose under this hood and I'll bite you!

She heard Nona pick the radio up from the floor; well, she would do that, the radio.

'It's my rattle,' she said to throw her.

'Min says her radio's rattling. Reception is rather poor.'

You can rock yourself in a pram, the glory of wheels.

'They wheeled him out.'

IX

'Of an evening' the Salle St Anne: the retreatants' sitting room with its huge bay windows looking out over the Atlantic.

A large room, demonstrably a victim of many charitable sales of work. Too many chairs – there always had been: relics from the Belgian Congo, of an evening, sometimes even Monsieur le Directeur himself. The sagging Dralon suite, the copper-covered coffee table someone's nephew made at school. The rag rugs and the orange and pink turf basket, an upright piano covered with a fringed and faded lozenge-patterned chenille cloth. The library corner with its convent collection covered in wallpaper scraps: *Francis of Assisi*, *The Little Flower*, appearances of the BVM. *Lord of the Flies*, Iris Murdoch, John Julius Norwich on Tuscany, Cotswold walks and this year a spanking row of new paperbacks bought by Rachel who wears Ireland like a grass skirt: *Life on the Blasketts*, *Island Man*, *Peig*, a glossy catalogue from the Uffizi Gallery abandoned between Cluedo, Monopoly and L'Attaque. A puzzle of Versailles and, over 1000 pieces, 'The Laughing Cavalier'; Richard's copy of *The Collectors' A to Z*, various newspapers, Eileen's pile of *Ireland's Own*.

Too many chairs, but so far west the light lingers long in the evenings, concealing for an hour or two the drabness of the room. In the warm glow, the fading light, it's beautiful. In the long western twilights the room comes into its own: the lozenged cloth covering the piano complements the pokerwork fire screen and goes, quite nicely thank you, with the Dralon suite and the green wing-back chair with its cover of hunting scenes. The baize of the card table with its four corner ashtrays like billiard pockets – even Monsieur le Directeur likes a smoke; a reflection on the surface of the copper table of Rachel's Spanish guitar. For an hour or two on a summer night there is harmony in this room – until Richard comes into it, destroys the illusion, switches on the electric light. Then it's afternoon again, or morning, bright light, hard light; now it's trouble with the guttering and damp patches on the walls and the small door which leads out to the garden and *The Bliss* swollen and distorted by the wet. The black leather-look director's swivel chair is hideous and mended with masking tape on the seat; the piano, forlorn beneath its drooping cover, looks out of place, like a piece of furniture abandoned temporarily in a move. Reception is poor on the radio, the books look boring, the puzzles have all been done.

'We make our own amusement, Julia.'

X

The nuns are filing into chapel. There is a slight hold-up for Sister Agnes, making progress slowly with her walking frame. Sister Basil has entered chapel first; the other sisters follow on, progressing, hands joined, down the wide thoroughfare of the trunk road, making little of themselves, the humble effacing of self along the edges of the corridor. Rachel passes with exaggerated quietness on the other side and even before their black figures have disappeared into the twilight of the chapel there is the sense, always the sensation, of very few people about.

In the kitchen Eileen irons to the sound of RTE Radio 1: 'Dance yourself dizzy to Joe Dolan, tonight at the Abbey Glen Hotel'. 'Meet the gang. Make that date to disco at Dooneen's.' She thumps the board in front of her as reception comes and goes; Rachel's had a go at it for her but in her hands only Raidio na Gaeltachta comes out clear.

Though large, the kitchen is a homely place but Rachel's made the radio fuzzy and Eileen's in a mood. She raises her eyes to heaven and brings them to rest automatically on the lighter rectangle of pale green eggshell paint where the print of the *Sacred Heart of Jesus* used to hang. Nona had noticed that straight off: 'A vast improvement, Eileen'; Jesus in the kitchen had never looked quite right. Julia had a corkboard in her kitchen, a corkboard with glass-headed pins: fitness sessions, fringe events, babysitting circle, Oliver's monthly orthodontal appointment card, lest we forget.

'I'd love a corkboard,' Eileen said. She'd love a lot of things.

Outside the door, among the calor gas bottles that Jim had promised he would help her lift, the island's population of stray cats clawed and fought. Jesus! She was late and the ironing was late too. She had a period coming, she dreaded it; her stomach clenching into a great big knot, like what would happen if you swallowed chewing gum. The doctor says, she told Nona, that what's needed is for her to have a child. Stuck this side of the mountains, the Twelve Bens, there's a fat chance of anything like that.

She'd love a corkboard. She begged Sylvester to take her to Dooneen's. Mary Doris is off to Boston but with the likes of her in America Eileen might as well stay put. She'd like some pin-heel shoes. She's off ironing; she'd like to put her feet up and just sleep.

Unlike other women – Rachel, Nona – she has difficulty doing more than one thing at a time and when she dreams she scorches: God save us, a great brown singe mark on the pillow slip. She stuffs it into the compost bucket – no good for anything but to be chucked. Five minutes now and her father will be over for her; no privacy in this kitchen with or without the

47

Sacred Heart. In her opinion, seldom sought, it's the nuns' private parts that keeps them sensible. Privacy in this kitchen is a joke.

XI

Not dark till nearly eleven, but the lighthouse sweeps
its beam from Ross's Point to Muckinish, Moynismore,
Currickluhan, Cuddoo, Feroonagh. The coast revealed
winds in and out like a crazy lampshade fringe.

Dark in the convent, a pulse of light plays across
Min's ceiling. 'Give light to these eyes before they close
in death': her prayer to the beat of the beam. 'Take me
back to the plateau and let me lie there like a rabbit
full out in the sun. If I must go all unremembered let
me remember –

    In the corner of a house without roof or window
    In the gable end out of the wind.

There, then gone again, the light sweeps over the hen
houses and down to the Chesterfield arms of the maze.
Richard prays:

Holy shroud, winding cloth
I feel it more than Min
Our Father, my step-father
A greasy little Frenchman of whom I felt ashamed.
My step-father, knocked me sideways
Affected my health, made it impossible.
Arrest my hypochondria! Hear my prayer!
Been on my own too long, since my mother, Bernard,
water under the bridge.
Marking time a bit since those days, shock to the
system, all that.
A deal between us, not before time, the gardening and
the inkwells are for you.
Played fly-half, fit as a fiddle,
Mother lined my trousers if they itched.
Turned up at Sports Day, her arm in his arm, out of
the bleeding blue.
Member of the chorus in the Greek play, learnt my
lines for her
But her arm in his arm, after the performance, went off
on my own.
Mother and I, long before Bernard, part of team you
see.
I repent! I repent!
Not about Bernard but about the years that, because of
him, I've wasted.
I repent of all the many autumns of my life alone.
The autumns when I did not divide up bedding plants
or heel in wallflowers
Winter lettuces! Brought in for Rachel. Please God
grant me that.
Talking to Rachel, through a kitchen window, plans
for winter lettuces
And early beans and peas.

*

On the opposite shore the lights are blazing. Eileen's in bed with a hottie, Sylvester and her father sit on in the bar, whilst in town they're dancing themselves dizzy at Dooneen's.

Alone in the lounge part of the bar, distinguished by lampshades and carpets, the small colour television on top of the piano, the silk flowers on top of the television, the religious calendar – 'Yet a little time is the light with you; walk while you have the light' – Joe Reihill takes a drink or two with Sylvester and defends the purchase, on the HP, of the brand-new computerised till. The tables have had their perfunctory wipe, the cloth sits on the bar. Sylvester won't stand still to listen to Joe's troubles, emptying ashtrays, sweeping up. His energy is unflagging, as befits a younger, more optimistic man. Only this afternoon Sylvester had arranged the shop so that Joe can't walk down any aisle without barking his poor old shins.

'America is nearer than you think,' he tells his cousin Joe.

Joe says, 'So what possessed you to come back?'

In the convent the nuns keep the big silence. Min feels she can almost hold on to it, it is so tangible to her. The beam on her ceiling shines on Jim who has missed his lift from town and is walking it, making his way to Carneys' barn.

Too old for this sort of caper. Never worry, the barn would be dry and, in a way he couldn't quite put words to, he liked to be out and to know about the night. Sometimes he had a drop too much and sometimes he had a drop too little; most times he had a drop on him just to keep out the worst. They said about him that he drank because he'd made mistakes and messed his life up, or that he'd made mistakes and messed his life up because he drank. He drank because they talked about him. Drink made him notorious but in its own way brought anonymity as well. In drink the path was swept and cleared; possibilities, concealed from him in the sober state, miraculously emerged. When he drank he turned his story over in his head and considered Min's place in all of it. Without her, even in drink, he foresaw a future that held few possibilities at all.

Right up until his late twenties he'd lived with his mother and done odd jobs. At one time there had been a van. When she died on him he went away to the town to an uncle who'd been after him for some time. With mother not around to take his money off him and an uncle who paid cash into his hand, the rot set in. The women weren't that stuck on him – a lot of them went to America, others had their heads turned by tourists, the best of them stayed and married young; with full board at his uncle's he had nothing to spend his money on but drink. He could imitate a seagull and a chorus of barking dogs and he played the entertainer in the bars. He could make his knees crack and his thumbs wiggle, he could touch his nose with the tip of his tongue – assets more in demand than his imitations, for who cared for a performance of a dog barking, running after a car, when the real thing was so near at hand? His ear was good and his real talent was for the piano, but he'd been out of luck with that. The last bar with live music in it changed when he was living at his uncle's and when it came back again and he caught on to what was happening he was too frayed at the edges by alcohol to be taken on for anything like that. Twice he was banned from driving, but it didn't succeed in stopping him using the van, which could be seen by the Gardai parked outside his mother's cottage – which by this time had become a tip. The van was a tip, too: the bag of tools, chip papers, newspapers, beer cans, bottles – you could hardly negotiate the front seats of it, let alone the back. When it was discovered with him inside it, having driven right off the sky road and into the corners of Carneys' barn where he now quite peacefully slept, they said he was lucky to be alive. He was. He got it towed back from there to the cottage but the sump was gone, the front smashed and the lights buggered, and he sold the engine to pay for the price of the tow. There were still bits of it that were of use; the seats he took out and put in the bit of wasteland that was his garden, the carcase was lifted up and into a sand dune near the beach, an eyesore among other eyesores, and now the dogs sat in it, the papers blown out of it long since through the shattered quarter-light. Ah now, he missed the driving, he'd been really fond of the van.

After the uncle he moved to a sister of his mother's at Moyard, worked at the marble at Streamstown which he hated and soon left. Odd jobs seemed the better bet for him and the years passed, working on the bungalows at Auchrisbeg and Knockavilra and, in the summer, doing a little in the fields. He tried to sell his cottage to the Germans but by then it had gone too far. He took lodgings in the town, not with the uncle this time but with the librarian, who, everyone knew it, was soft. But not that soft, for when work was scarce the librarian booted him out in favour of someone with regular employ. The aunt in Moyard put him back on the marble and was forced to apologise for him when once again he upped and left. In the end it was she who, in desperation, contacted the nuns of Inishcara and they, the Sisters of the Brick, who gave him the nearest he got to a permanent home.

Now he stocked groceries at Reihill's, drank in the bar, did any odd jobs going. The nuns couldn't pay him but they gave him a roof over his head. So it was at the age of fifty-three but looking older, he was back almost where he came from and could be said, in the context of this sort of life, to have finally settled down. He still tried to sell his cottage, although the dogs had been in by now and the donkeys and the sheep. He'd thoughts of renting it through Bord Failte, but the inspector who came out to visit left quite shocked; declared himself quite appalled by the state of the old cottage. Too close to the bone, he said, too reminiscent of the real thing.

He slept late at Carneys' and the cash and carry stuff had already been unloaded by the time he made it to Reihill's and there was nothing for it but to steady himself with a drink. He could hear Reihill and his wife in the front room eating. He joined Sylvester in the bar.

Sylvester was a great man in Jim's opinion and a great one for the crack. He divided his time between Connemara and up around Sligo and the north. Jim had a Paddy and watched Sylvester optimistically ring the sale up on the impressive computerised till. The silence was companionable, for though Sylvester was a youngster compared with Jim he was a man with a good attitude; he got on with things and seemed to be happy anywhere he went. These days Sylvester had an edge to his voice, a voice with corners on it, different from the local lilt: they teased him about it on his annual visits – he was popular in the bar.

'Good on you Jim,' he said. 'Were you in England?'

'I was.'

'When would that be then?'

'In the winter, you know, over for a bit I was.'

'And what are you at now?' Sylvester asked him, knowing only too well.

Jim nodded his head in the direction of Inishcara.

'At the convent are you? That so. And what is it you're doing over there?'

Jim waved a trembling hand, signifying this and that. He saw his own reflection in the bar mirror: 'We all adora Kia-Ora.' Even at this time of the morning Sylvester was excellently turned out; he had money, obviously.

'Are you staying yourself?' Jim asked, also knowing the reply.

'Down for the wee holiday.'

Jim admired Sylvester, he really did. Sylvester's holidays had little in common with the rigorous leisure pursuits of the Germans and English who took the cottages and gave the bar and shop their trade. His holiday was a working one, behind the bar. He looked at his own reflection again, squared his shoulders and drank his Paddy down as fast as he knew how. Ordered one up again. 'And have one for yourself.'

'Still got the house, Jim?'

'I have.'

'Standing up is it?'

'It is surely.'

'You're not staying in it, then?'

'Sure it's no good to me without the van.'

'Ah.'

They drank.

'On your feet are you?'

'I am for now, like.'

'Earning good money over there though?'

'I am not.'

'How's that?'

'I've food and board just.'

'Not the same, is it?' Sylvester sympathised, looking at the so-far unpaid-for drinks.

55

'It is not.'

They sat for a while and thought about it.

The till was an impressive sight; it seemed to get bigger as Jim looked at it, as it dawned on both of them that he had nothing to put in it.

'You have the hang of that contraption Sylvester?'

'I have surely.'

'What happened the old one?'

'Joe traded it.'

'Money makes money.'

'It does. And there's no way you can get the money wrong on this one.'

'Is that so?'

'Foolproof,' said Sylvester.

The till was big, the bar was very empty.

'Not many people about this year,' Jim commented.

'Not much money about now.'

'There is not.'

The holidaymakers rarely drank during the day, but most evenings now the bar was fairly full. The English seemed to bring their licensing laws with them; the Germans took bottles of beer and wine on picnics and fishing trips.

'A bad summer.'

'Terrible altogether.'

The bell went in the shop then and without any hurry Sylvester went off to see to it. Jim stared into his drink.

'One of your lot, the little dark one, Australian. Not bad-looking, Jim boy.'

Jim was feeling uneasy now, without his breakfast.

'Sure, I bet you're having a great time over yonder,' Sylvester teased him, 'looking at the likes of her.'

Jim nodded.

'I bet they're all after it, aren't they, Jimmy?'

'I don't know.' Jim's hands were steadier than they had been but now he felt a little sick.

'Come on, course they are, and you not too old to give it to them, so I've heard. You ought to get in there, boyo – probably all dying for it, so they are! Loaded with cash aren't they? Do you not fancy yourself as a kept man Jim?'

'Are you a kept man?'

'Away with you – I can barely keep myself.' But Sylvester looked great; it was just his way of going on. Jim felt old and shabby next to the likes of him. The bell went in the shop once more.

'A bit of it whenever you fancy it,' Sylvester said.

XII

Min remembered. It was a day of squalls, the weather coming up from all directions, a strong gusting wind; May, but little sign of spring. She was working upstairs in the nuns' chambrettes. Peace to be found in the lack of individuality, no clue to personality: these women with varied tastes and backgrounds, of different nationalities, inhabited their similar cells without leaving a trace or a mark. She changed the sheets, competent now with the ritual folding of the quilts and blankets. The mean curtains blew out of the open windows, the intoxication of the polish on the bedside tables and the curtains blowing out, the sea all up in flowers and swirls that morning: exhilaration as far as the eye could see. The rag rugs made by the sisters were turned each morning so that even something so cheap and meagre faded equally on both sides. On Fridays she took the mats out to beat them, catching them by the four corners as she'd been taught by Sister Agnes so that the dust and fluff was not trailed down the stairs, even the back stairs . . .

As she walked through the quiet back of the house she could hear how the wind was hitting it; the pat, pat of a door not properly closed somewhere, the bang, bang, bang. They were building the German bungalow around then, waist high, creeping in a corner of the mainland shore. The convent stood to be knocked down and she was proud of it; the wind licked at it, the salt corroded, the rain seeped in. In those days, too, there was singing in the kitchen and no radio and the *Sacred Heart* bled above the door where Min stepped out with the mats.

She stacked them on the dry stone of the porch, then out she went with them, one by one, the mats flying straight out in front of her. She had to hold on tight, the noise outside of the waves pounding into the island, breaking white beyond the lighthouse, raging from Ross's Point, roaring past Inishcara, raising spray as far inland as Booters Bay. The mats flew, the wet slapped at her face, the wind got into her ears and made her nose run, her eyes smart, her overall blew against the back of her legs; reluctantly she brought each one in. It was on the last mat with the first excitement of the weather over that she realised she was being watched. Jim.

'Were you ever at an ice rink?' he asked her.

'What?'

In the wind and weather it was hard to catch what he was saying. She moved with him back into the shelter of the porch.

'Ice skating, you know?'

She looked up at him and laughed, the mats in her arms dustless and damp and her eyes unguarded, sparkling.

'Were you then?'

'Well, a long time ago.'

'Would you try it again, like?' He laughed with her, as if he knew it was a strange way of going about things. Their laughter went up in the wind and blew round them, he with his bag beneath his arm, her with the mats.

XIII

Min's oldest friend, all that, Nona, here to cope. Only a matter of time and time on Nona's hands – not remotely busy. Appalling weather – 'Unusual, Julia, even over here'; no entries in the visitors book thus far. A splendid opportunity to spend more time with Min. A different Min.

Nona saw to the visiting rota, tried to be as diplomatic as possible with Eileen on the prickly subject of Min's diet. Eileen had her hands full, too busy to note a marked reluctance in Nona to spend time with Min. Eileen sensed nothing, Rachel did – mercifully, and for the moment Rachel had taken the wrong tack. The contrast between a grisly life on earth and a glorious, fun-filled, sun-kissed, in-shouting-distance-of-Our-Redeemer existence in heaven was underlined by her selection of mealtime readings at the lectern. Later, in the Salle, she took time to expand for Nona's benefit on what she called 'the convent's attitude to death'. Min was about to embark on her greatest journey, well-prepared by Monsieur le Directeur, well on her way to something better, somewhere else. 'Life's unimportant, Nona, in comparison to death'; and, sensing still that Nona had some qualms about it, offered further palliatives: that Min 'was very muddled' although 'virtually free from pain'.

Rot.

Nona sat and struggled by Min's bed.

'How does the rota suit you, dear?' Min's silence made her nervous, made her own voice sound bossy and loud. 'Always a good idea to have things evenly spaced. One visit in the morning, another in the afternoon, another after supper?'

It did not occur to Nona – why should it have? – that nights and days were one now for Min, that day, that morning, noon and evening had become an arbitrary thing. And then when you're dying, Nona thought, we'll go into another gear; whatever happens you mustn't worry about a thing. Rachel and the sisters, Eileen, Richard and I – the baton of visits and requests passed on.

'Your days must be fairly full up, dear,' she said. 'Now I knew I had something to ask you. Do you really want Jim in to mend this window? It's a bit of bother, don't you think?'

'Yes.'

'Yes, you don't?'

'He's good at it.'

'Well.' Actually Nona found him less than thorough but she agreed with Min. It didn't do to disagree with the sick – one left out the normal cut and thrust.

Min was quiet again.

'Are you feeling rotten, Min? Just a bad day, is it?'

'You woke me up.'

'You were just waking, dear, as I came in.'

'I wasn't up till now.'

'What? You're depressed this morning, Min. You mustn't get depressed. A better quilt would cheer things up in here. If Eileen can't put her hand on one no one can.'

'No one can.'

'What dear?'

Depressed.

Silence. And Nona left to cast about for something else to say. Possibly the only advantage of Min's travel plans was the handbag now hanging over the edge of her bed. The saga of that handbag – how it slipped under sofas and turned up in the turf basket, how it hid in between the cushion and the arm of various chairs, the handbag brought in by tutting sisters left out all night in the rain, the handbag in the linen basket, the handbag left in town, the search parties organised at the last minute to find that bag . . . Nona had often wondered what was in it that was so precious.

'The number of times you lost that bag!'

She wasn't even up to losing things any more; the only thing left to lose was consciousness.

'Now I meant to say to you yesterday, is there anyone you'd like me to write to, Min? We didn't hear from your sister-in-law now, did we?'

No we didn't because Eileen didn't post it because I asked her not to. Nona. The letters she wrote on Min's behalf were a scream. Letters like news flashes, letters like alarm calls: 'Will Mrs Rigsby, believed to be living in the Channel Islands, contact her sister-in-law Margaret Warner who is dangerously ill?' And dangerously bored.

63

Richard and Rachel came together, worse than dull.

'Shall we try again, Min?'

'What?'

'I think we ought to, don't you?'

Ought to, another 'ought'. Put that down on the list of 'oughts'. She ought to answer Nona but if she didn't perhaps Nona would go away. Nona was going on about it. Min didn't like her sister-in-law; perhaps the sister-in-law was dead. Robert wasn't dead: someone would have told her, written like Nona wanted to write for Min. She wanted to giggle when she thought of Nona's letters. Life was silly but illness was very serious indeed.

'Richard's knot garden's coming on well.'

Richard and Rachel, the terrible twins of boredom.

'It'll be lovely when it grows up.'

'I won't see it.'

'Of course you will.'

Liar.

'You mustn't be morbid, Min.'

It seemed sensible in the circumstances.

'Being morbid won't get you anywhere.'

Out of the lay-by on to the bypass.

This was an early visit. Looking back on it a few days later, it seemed almost easy-going, normal, for more and more Nona dreaded turning off the trunk road to that little downstairs room. Sometimes Min wouldn't talk to her at all; Nona talked, Min listened but not in the old way, the proper way ... Nona had always talked to Min; Min was her sounding board. Nona told her all her news, Min was the person Nona spoke to in her talks, and it might sound immodest but Min had always looked up to Nona, not least because Nona was – well, in comparison to Min she was – a woman of the world.

Now when Nona talked Min just stared at her. That look. Disapproving and, in a disconcerting way, superior; it was hard to forget that look. When she did talk it was trivia and it was talked *at* Nona, not *to*. Only the other day Min had cut into what Nona was telling her in a most unexpected, uncharacteristic way. She started talking some nonsense about having to put a paraffin heater in an outside lavatory, gone on and on about it, leaving Nona to say what were Min's lines surely, 'How interesting, do go on.'

'She's very muddled.'

Not as muddled as all that.

Why did she do it? What did she mean by it? The atmosphere in that little room was so unpleasant. 'Awful Julia!' Was this what people meant when they said that sitting with the sick was so upsetting? And she dared not ask the others what they thought. Min was vindictive: Nona saw it in her eyes, she could not forget that look. It lingered. Nona could leave Min's room quite easily: one just stood up, offered some excuse and left. Easy, but even then there was a sense that Min was winning because the excuse was fabricated, you'd lied. Easy to get away and yet so difficult. Min would not leave her; that stare stayed with you. Illness was awful and upsetting and could not be contained by the simple shutting of the sick-room door.

How did the others fare, she wondered? It would be almost worthwhile listening at the keyhole just to put her mind at rest. She asked Eileen, who replied that they talked about shopping. This seemed innocuous enough. She might try shopping next time but, surely, if time was really short, they ought to talk about something more suitable, about God or Robert . . . To spend your days talking about paraffin heaters, about shopping – a death on this level made life seem absurd, made perming one's hair pointless after all. She wished she could discuss it with someone. Monsieur le Directeur was the obvious choice but she couldn't talk to him about it, wouldn't trust him not to tell.

If Min was unfulfilled or something, well, it wasn't down to her. 'We can hardly be held responsible for each other, can we?' she said to Abraham in the lodge. Abraham's face looked down on Nona, a sneer embedded in his beard. On close inspection his eyes were Min's eyes. She turned her face away.

'So that's it, is it?' she said later. 'The eyes have it.'

Eyes that pass their burden, Min's eyes, day by day and piece by piece; Nona felt that she would never now be free of her discovery, would wear it like a stone around her neck.

'Shake it off like a cold, Mother.' Julia was absolutely right: work was the obvious solution. She knew it, but was disappointed that it had to come to that. Normally she had a complete rest. She hoped that ideas might come and sometimes on her holidays had felt frustrated that she was unable to find the time to sort them out. Holidays on Iniscara were far too much fun to work in, but Richard was preoccupied with the knot garden . . .

To convince herself as much as anyone Nona had told Rachel an insignificant white lie. A producer, Andrew Baxter. No perhaps Rachel hadn't heard of him – who had? Well, he'd begged and finally persuaded her to make this visit to Inishcara slightly more of a working holiday than most. Rachel's anorexic experiences would flesh out an article already substantially researched: could Rachel find the time to help her, some afternoon perhaps?

'Fine by me if we can do it in the morning, Nona. I like to garden in the afternoons and there's not much happening in the lodge.'

'Well.'

' 'Course if you don't want your space invaded . . .'

'Spoice?'

'You could always lock up for a moment – we could do it over coffee in the kitchen.'

'I don't think so, dear, I like to do things properly' – she stopped herself saying, I am a professional; that went without saying – 'I don't think I can really interview you in the kitchen, dear.'

'In the lodge then, OK?'

It wasn't OK at all.

She willed herself to relax. First the photograph of Rachel at her brother's wedding.

'I was just like a stick, Nona, believe me a lead pencil. If I did eat I made myself vomit.'

She was eating now, Nona noticed, chewing gum.

'I'd always been fairly underdeveloped for my age, you see, Nona, and no one noticed what was really happening.'

'Insidious,' Nona wrote down, but not so Rachel could see the word. She didn't look underdeveloped now; Eileen told her that in one good week in June she had taken her top off on the strand.

'And no one had any idea of what I was feeling inside, you see – the torment. I was going round the bend, Nona, no two ways about it. I was in hell.'

'And then you,' – how easy it was to catch the cliché with Rachel – 'found God?'

'I did.'

Where? Nona wondered.

'You remember I told you back in May about my psychotherapist?'

Yes, Nona remembered. Those first conversations at the time when Nona had been showing Rachel Dixon the ropes, introducing her, helping her feel at home; in this she had obviously succeeded. The gum chewer sprawled across the chair.

'The analyst. You were very fond of him?'

'I became dependent on him, Nona, there's no other word for it really. You're supposed to work through that feeling of dependence but I got stuck. Like a drug! I just projected everything on to the poor guy. I wanted to be with him: not just appointments, all the time. I hung around outside his office, I wanted to live in his pocket.'

His trouser pocket?

'I was making a proper fool of myself but I still felt so lost.'

'Surely your parents . . .?'

'My folks just couldn't reach me, Nona.'

'I see.'

'Oh you don't see, you don't see. Believe me, Nona, it's madness! This great gap between you and the folks who love you most and you're trying to kill yourself, working against yourself to make the gap even greater. I realise now that wanting to kill yourself is not simply about the parental gap but the gap between you and God. That guy was everything to me.'

God? Nona had hardly written anything in her notebook. She studied the empty page. The nerves of earlier that morning had left her, the rain coursed down against the windows, she toyed with the cord on her glasses, she felt supreme.

'So what exactly did these sessions with your . . . psychotherapist entail?'

'I went over there every day except the weekend. I

drove myself. I could call him any time on a help line but I didn't always get him and I wasn't going to talk to anyone else, so for me the weekends were pretty hell. I had two hours with him every day.'

'And what happened?'

'Most of the time we talked, I talked. Then there were these wonderful silences – it's not easy to explain. He seemed to look right into me, you know, tell me with his eyes that what he saw there was good. Silences were golden moments, meaningful, you know? He was always so pleased to see me. I knew I could say anything to him, anything I wanted; things I didn't even know I wanted to say came out. I really opened up to him. He was there for me: for the first time in my life I could really talk to someone, there was no shame.'

'Shame,' wrote Nona. Rachel had already told her in some detail about the quality and quantity of her shame: pubescent shame – 'I just didn't want to face up to being a woman, None'; parental shame – 'Mum had been in analysis, too. It started as a dust allergy. Then I guess she came to think of dust in a more symbolic way: I was dust, she hated me, she was jealous. My puberty challenged her you see . . .'

'I could have died if it wasn't for that guy, Nona, I know that now. It's a debt I can't ever repay: I owe my life to him!'

Nona relished the faint but discernible note of hysteria in Rachel's tone. Rachel was no challenge to her, pubescent or mature.

'And your present relations with your . . . folks? Your mother?'

'Really only so so, None. I don't think she's over dust and she really doesn't know God closely. She lives her life without him, you see, she won't let him in.'

'That's a gulf between you?'

'One helluva gulf, Nona. A great big hole.'

Nona left the silences unfilled. She felt curiously unmoved. Julia crossed her field of vision but she ignored her too.

'I'm going to build a bridge, Nona,' Rachel was saying. 'I'm going to bridge that gulf.'

'I'm sure you are.'

'I'm sure I am. He will give me strength to do it.'

He. Nona was starving. Rachel had chewed almost constantly throughout the interview. Perhaps it was talking about anorexia that made Nona look forward more than usual to her lunch. This thin young woman seemed to get food everywhere; spiritual snacks from God, gum from her pockets. Beneath 'shame' Nona wrote down 'greed'.

The interview continued in the same vein until it was cut short by the arrival of Monsieur le Directeur's car, a cue for Rachel to ditch the confidences of the morning and get out. 'Insidious, shame, greed'; Nona had the sudden urge to write 'bitch'.

The heavy scent of patchouli lingered in the room but Nona left the window closed, knowing of old that if she opened it, it stuck. Jim had re-hung the kitchen door, she hadn't seen much of him this August, wondered how long it would be before he got round to her. In May it had sounded as if they were getting the lot done; perhaps the money hadn't yet come through. There had been changes of a different sort all instigated by Rachel. This young woman, this lead pencil, had actually written her name all over the convent in one way or another: topless bathing, religious readings. She heard Rachel laughing outside her window. Monsieur le Directeur was not renowned for his wit. They had something in common of course, these two, they had Him.

70

Him. Rachel said He gave her energy; with Him she was unstoppable, she said. Up in the middle of the night for prayers, early Mass when there was one, beating everyone to the breakfast table, Benediction, helping in the kitchen, helping in the garden, taking her top off on the strand. She said that she'd been cruel to her body and now celebrated it, and now must give it love. She had nail varnish in her chambrette and conditioner, patchouli dabbed behind the ears and wrists. 'Listless, unmotivated, rudderless, aimless' was how she had described her early self to Nona, 'dependent, despondent, suicidal'. Nona felt tense again; her foot waggled furiously beneath the table. 'We are all going swimming together,' she'd said. Really, since when? Organised bathing, religious readings, knot gardens . . .

Aerobics, evangelical handclapping, tossing the health food loaf. 'All things on your corkboard, Julia.'

'Everything you go to Ireland to get away from, Mum.'

XIV

Jim ran the water which came out, brown and cloudy, boiling into the bath. As the place filled up with steam drops of condensation formed where the ceiling met the walls.

He removed his ropey assortment of clothes, paused for a moment to check a blackened thumb. His mind hadn't been concentrating right when he did that. Steam and condensation. The room was small and badly built; whoever hung and grouted the tiles behind the basin wasn't concentrating either. The room had been an office before retreatants became a feature of the convent: 'Office' remained written on the door. Start in the middle and work sideways was the rule for tiling and I, he thought, have been middle and sideways all my life.

The amount of talk that had been going round his head! It seemed like forever. He ran water into the basin now, depressed was not a word in his vocabulary: he felt 'down'. He had ambitions and anxieties like the rest of them but there was really no one he could talk to who hadn't labelled him years since as 'no go'. 'Talking away to myself.' He checked that the door was truly locked before removing his underpants to soak them in the basin.

Eileen wanted this moved and that shifted and this out from under her feet – everyone he saw these days gave him another job. To do what he wanted to do, to get his house done up and move Min in there, dribs and drabs of money, egg money off Eileen, he needed big money to do that. Big money. And he'd never had big money, never, because his mother said, his aunt said, his uncle said he was soft. Soft to bring some rotten thing, some ill creature in to die, soft because he had no idea of organisation, because he left everything too late.

He turned the taps off, returned to the basin, poked the pants. He rubbed a clearing in the mirror; he had to bend his knees to look in it. 'I have my hair at least.' He patted his hair: it had quirks in it, the result of a double-crown which made his hair cross over itself and get awkward. It only looked something damped down a bit or wet. Still he left the bath and got his toothbrush out of his bag. 'Teeth aren't bad either.' He didn't brush but ran a nicotine-stained finger over the teeth; the contrast was a good one, the teeth were very white. Fine teeth. He left the pants to soak and lowered himself – the whole of life was an awkward space – lowered himself into the short, narrow bath.

The long, old body. It was confidence that he lacked. His face and forearms were ruddy with a red triangle where his shirt was open; the rest of his body, still with muscle on it from years of outside work, was

73

newborn-looking, soft white. Better-looking in clothes than out of them, looking again at the locked door, anxious about his nakedness. He washed thoroughly and then lay for a long time thinking, slipping the bar of soap from red hand to red hand.

'Your mother. Maybe she hadn't a lot to give you but she couldn't have loved you more. You, Jim. Worried sick about you. Your mother would have wanted you to find a nice girl and settle down with her.' His aunt told him all this. Told him, told him, warned him even, told him but never told him how. As it was, then and now, he'd never been the type to impress anyone's mother and then the girls he'd been with in his youth acted as if they didn't have mothers anyway. 'A nice girl', Margaret — he liked to call Min by her real name, 'Margaret' — would have impressed his mother and his aunty, impressed them all. His Margaret, different despite what Sylvester said about all women being the same — on about the women at the convent, wanting it, all that. He remembered the first day he spoke to her. The way she'd laughed then wasn't ordinary: she laughed with relief like he'd opened a box for her, let her out. Let her out; but now he couldn't, now it was too late. Not depressed but low that August evening; why reveal to him what love was? Why let him know that love was a great thing? Let him feel it, let him know it but not let him have it to keep?

Marriage was not the same as love. He'd no thoughts on the subject, really, despite the teachings of the Church. Even in his youth, and the urgings from his aunty, he'd felt instinctively that marriage thoughts did not apply to him. You went with someone for a while like, or you picked girls up at dances and these were, Sylvester Reihill, the women that you talk about, the women all the same. They wouldn't let you do it or they said they didn't want to or couldn't, and if you did then they had something on you and wouldn't let you go. He wouldn't be a normal man if he hadn't had his leg over now and again with women like that, but love had nothing to do with it at all. Before Margaret he'd never slept with a woman in a bed for one thing – rather, if they'd stayed with him he'd woken up beside them in a stinking car. How it evaporated, that feeling you had for them, after it was done! He'd had no trouble, really, if it came to counting heads, so he knew that it wasn't just that she was English made her different, for he'd been around a lot of English tourists here, and Germans, he knew it wasn't that.

Why show him what it was, then? Why hurt him with it? Let him feel it and know it, not let him have it to take home?

XV

'We make our own amusement, Julia.' That night Jim played the piano for them in the Salle.

Cleaned up, shaven, his long back bent over the piano, sloping shoulders, the sleeves of his jacket, and Richard noticed, ending well before the flying fingers, jumping wrists. He looked at nothing when he played because the music was all in his head: Paul McCartney, Mario Lanza – he'd got them all by ear. They loved it when he played for them – he could see it on their faces. Their faces, Margaret's face, in that chill, north-facing room with its electric lights now blacking out all but the memory of the sea.

When the requests were over Richard, Nona, Eileen and Rachel played whist and then canasta, cards falling on the baize table, cigarettes burning in the corner ashtrays and he, rolling up a cigarette himself, swinging the long bent legs out from under the piano, watching. Later he played again more quietly and as he played, the secret inside him, churned up in the bath, settled itself right in. Only Richard spoke to him much that evening; there was no talking to the man; he had all the words and clever phrases, the words that always wrote Jim off.

XVI

A nun looked in on Min, blessed her and gently closed the door. Silence again after faint music. Min remembered . . . those weeks after they'd first spoken. Weeks that she thought of as a Saturday here, a Monday, a Tuesday. She watched the sky as she had always done, seeing the clouds build from the upstairs window and the rain over the Atlantic or sun on the mainland and rain round *The Bliss*, and the eyes like stones that she'd kept where she wanted them all the years since she'd left England strayed around the gardens and the ear listened for something new in the sisters' house.

Jim was about, replacing windows, pointing the stonework. If she heard him in any direction she would walk the other way: his hum and his muttering in the corridors in this quiet house. He was a messy worker and she tidied after him. He took brushes from the cupboard and put them back outside it; she busied herself with that. He swept his mess into piles in the corners – he never used the dustpan or the little brush. She came upon signs of him like one did an animal: a piece of sandpaper that had been folded over a block of wood. She picked them up, dreaming; here was a rag and a block of wood, the chisel and the wedge of his conversation breaking in. Thinking about him had made her think at last of her early life and the house she'd left behind long ago. That Christmas, the matching watercolours in the hall, where she'd stood in a fur coat hugging a hot-water bottle, the box of decorations overflowing on the trolley and her hand plunged deep into it for the tinsel; and how, then, she had decided that she had to go. Quite suddenly she knew that among many other things she loathed, hated, wanted to smash and smash were Robert's wishy-washy watercolours in the hall. That this was it and she would never again hang tinsel round the frames of *Wellington College from the Lakes* or, particularly, *A Corner of the Quadrangle, Wellington College.*

XVII

Min would talk to Eileen; she talked about her life. Her life and her mother's life. In the long afternoons Eileen sat in the basket chair in Min's room whilst she talked. What Min liked to do was to go shopping, to travel in her memory down the streets she'd known as a child and in and out of arcades and department stores in the days when she first married. Eileen accompanied her; they travelled together on what they called her 'treats'. Eileen, big-faced and capable, who let the ironing mount to spend time in Min's company, wouldn't let her fall and it didn't matter either how mundane one was with Eileen: Eileen coped with everything, nothing bored her, Eileen didn't mind. Min went off shopping, the thing she'd always loved to do. She amazed herself by what she could remember, especially of her childhood, and the very happy times before Robert was successful and the only period in her life that she had been poor.

'I used to buy pork griskins: they were the pieces of meat at the end of the fillet – lovely meat and very, very cheap. Next to the butcher there was a remnant shop at the back of a factory. I sewed a lot in those days; I had my mother's machine. I made everything that could be made from that material: "ends" they were called, which meant you had to be clever with the cutting. It wasn't sold on rolls, you bought it in pieces – you couldn't buy it by the yard. On Saturday mornings we used to shop together. Eleven or twelve we'd set out, after a little lie-in: the public library and food and buying things for the flat.'

Through Min, Eileen knew the butcher and the baker, who would and who wouldn't let Min put things by. She knew the flat that Min's mother so disapproved of, the bend on the stairs and the damp smell in the bedroom – always more noticeable when they returned after staying with his parents at weekends. The time Min had fallen down the area steps, slipped on a piece of ice: 'You feel awful when you fall, you know, even when you're still quite young.' The man who sold coal bricks; the family called the fatties who lived across the road from them and were always out in the street. Miles away from anywhere, together in this room, Eileen smelt the coal bricks, knew where Min bought the kindling bundles for her fire. 'On Sunday mornings the Salvation Army started off from the hostel down the road. The bells from all the city's churches – how delicious and how safe it was to lie listening in bed.' The internal view, the Brussels sprouts, the bread – and Eileen prompted her with questions, never let her fall. What colours did you wear then? How did you have your hair? What Min bought to wear at the Christmas party; she made it herself, the material not from the factory shop this time but from the fancy store down town. The only pattern that was anything like what she wanted was for a dress, halter-necked; she only bought the pattern for the top. Everyone wore long in those days, long as a matter of course.

Skating? Yes, she'd been skating. As a child she had learnt to do it in the blistering Februarys on the lake. Pushing a chair with runners on it, and to a rink with someone else's mother years ago. She hadn't enjoyed the rink: too much noise, too many children, bumping into you, grabbing hold; tugging your sweater (boleros Eileen!) linking arms, holding tight, pulling you down. Her father collected her; she had blisters on her feet and her wrist hurt. He'd been in a strange mood when she mentioned the old times, the first time, skating on the frozen pond and she could remember to this day how he'd told her that he was older now than his father had been when he died.

How old was her father? How old was his father when he died? About the same age as his grand-daughter, about the same age as Min? Richard and Nona were another generation, Eileen and Rachel another generation again, 28 days, 32 days, 35 days – numbers seemed to matter after all.

Those years ago she'd followed Jim discreetly round the house, her answer ready, quite rehearsed. Skating, love.

'I'm a bit rusty but I'll take a shot at it – I'll try.'

XVIII

Night; and the sheep turned away from the windows.
Dark and holy night. The closed piano, the empty
polished corridors, the pale green tongue-and-groove
partitions, the banister rails, the bedsteads, the plugs in
the basins and the teeth in the glass, waving antennae
on the alert now, all ears harkening to the confessions
of the night:

Mary most pure, Mary most chaste.

Chaster than Eileen who admits to impure thoughts by
the sackload and a sort of sin of omission concerning
the lift back from Dizzy Dooneen's. Her guardian angel
would help her and the mother of God be sure to
understand what she had wanted and what she had
been at. What with her doting so on her sister

Maureen's babies, both in the pram together, only eleven months between them, beautiful boy babies in lemon and light blue:

> Little ribbons
> Small buttons
> And the smell of babies.

> Seat of wisdom,

It did not seem rational to Nona that a man like Richard could spend so much time with a girl who got over-excited by a chive. No charisma to speak of, not much of a gardener; a girl, she had it on good authority, who took her top off on the beach.

'Aldwych,' she told the taxi driver.

'Miss Upton, do come in.'

'You know I've suffered, you know that I am the obvious choice.'

Memories of what she comes to Inishcara to forget: the running steps, the call in the corridor, 'Miss Upton, Miss Upton'. The wave from a young man running straight across a busy road.

'Miss Upton isn't it? Just the person I want to see. Now, do you know so-and-so's home address?'

Mystical Rose, tower of David, hedges of box,
Ark of the covenant, gate of heaven, Margaret and I,
The Cortina with the turquoise trim.
Refuge of sinners, cause of our joy, winter lettuces,
Wellington College from the lakes.
Comforter of the afflicted, health of the weak,
Mother of Julia, after the green light,
Babies in lemon and blue.

XIX

Joe Reihill rarely walked the five hundred yards or so from his bar and grocery down to the water's edge. This morning, though, he had to get away. The sun beamed over Iniscara, the tide swept in with its eight different currents covering each rock, hiding treachery, making the space between island and mainland clean again. Joe, in his St Bernard's anorak and slip-on shoes, studied the scum and the filth. 'Booters Bay' the children called it, this corner that Joe studied, the back of the sea's big cupboard; a car door, a kettle, bottomless buckets, boots, driftwood, a rusting cooker – not awe-inspiring any of it but easier to face than the monster in the lounge bar, the till. The till that did everything that could be done; that, diligently digital, held the memory – God, mother of God, forgive me – that takings had never been so far down. Ah now. The till would be the death of him, his downfall, a token of his foolishness, wasn't it, a display of how he, fifty if he's a day now, has to impress that cub Sylvester? Hadn't he pressurised the salesman into bringing it in the first place, wanting to get it in and settled like, before Sylvester was due down? Wanting to have something over Sylvester just this once, wanting to do something before Sylvester suggested it, wanting to show Sylvester that old Joe, though not a travelled man, has his finger on the pulse.

A monument to disaster: HP payments as long as your arm that he could well do without. 'Jesus wept!' He watched the water wash in and out of the old oven. Technology? Mother of God, give a man some rest. The government was full of it, that and the EEC – gave its mind to nothing else. He'd heard the arguments all right. How not having an industrial revolution they were moving straight into the technological one, turning it to their advantage, so they said. Sylvester would do well in the government: he was just like them – the same way of talking about things, pulling the wool, always turning things to advantage. There was nothing revolutionary about this view: obsolete domestic things rusting in the water, the little fields dotted with ruined hay, the legs of the cooker wedged into the sand – and hadn't he been trying in the same manner to keep his head above water, only that?

Finished, like everything else in Connemara, down the bloody pan. The nuns were off, upsticks; the old priest had taken his time in the telling of it, explaining what hardly needed to be explained, telling him the ins and the outs. Joe knew anyway; he'd had his suspicions. The priest was that long-winded, that keen on an audience, that used to being listened to, but it hadn't taken Joseph Reihill long to get the gist. Nuns on Iniscara were uneconomic, like his bloody till.

86

It was the impact, the old priest said, long overdue in these parts, the impact of the Pope's edict, Vatican II. Oh, it was all different now all right, all different now; nuns had the bit between their teeth now, just like any other women, and the mother house in Belgium wasn't the big place it used to be either but just a sort of dressing station now from which nuns, hard to credit, waltzed freely in and out. And Sylvester had been smarming all over the priest throughout this long talk, nodding in agreement. Joe waited for his cousin to ask him where he'd been all these years. 'Here,' he would have answered, thumping the bar between them, 'Here.'

The sisters of St Dymphna – even, would you credit it, skirts and jumpers, headscarfs – lived in ordinary houses now, saying mass on any old table, a power for good in the ghettoes, working with drug-users and fruit-machine addicts as far afield as Albuquerque and Amsterdam. And a lot of them had the education for it, qualified for all of it with degrees in social working and the like; psychologists they were now, counsellors, working alongside ordinary people, hardly distinguishable from anybody else. 'The mystery's all gone,' smarmed Sylvester and it seemed that it had, opened out and flattened like, like a cardboard box. There was more to the religious life these days, the priest said, more not less. More than prayers and saving souls. 'Change is a great thing,' Sylvester said, but loose change was a greater thing; and how was Joe to survive the loss of the convent, let alone the HP payments on the till? Oh, he'd chosen his time, the old priest, and he knew it too. Joe had never liked him: it was obvious that two children in a family didn't impress the man at all – this, when everyone knew his wife had problems and was lucky to be alive. Neither of his girls had entered the Church. You're either called or you're not, Joe protested, but it was obvious that the old man thought that his girls had been particularly cloth-eared in this respect. If more young girls had put themselves forward St Dymphna's might have gone on a good few years yet, he'd hinted, but what could a father persuade girls to do these days? Sure, girls had ideas of their own. Well. They couldn't support Eileen if she found herself out of a job and then what would she do? Nothing here except old boots, he mused, pretending to smile at a group of German fishermen, dressed like a showroom, wearing waders, launching a gleaming boat.

Technological revolution – what good was it to the people of the West? All these Germans came here to get away from it. Joe didn't get about much. He imagined Ireland fringed with tourists with nothing much in the middle apart from Dublin. Germans, English and Italians, picnicking around the Irish coast. What a year he'd had, what a year! He might have gone in for mackintoshes if he'd thought of it. There wasn't a cheap plastic mac to be had in town for love nor money, but it was too late in the season now to be starting anything like that. If he'd had an amusement arcade he'd have made some money; all he had was a miniature pool table, a television and a till. Mother of God, he couldn't look across the water without wishing he'd gone to America like the rest.

XX

The elephant remembers the ancient trackways
through the forest, forgets the movements of the tide.
Dressed for going to town, Nona stood looking through
her chambrette window at the water-covered strand.
Really! She was at sixes and sevens this August. Damn.
How could she have been so silly? She always went to
town around this point in her visit and it was Min's
fault, putting her off her stroke. She only wanted to go
to get away from Min and the worst of it was that she
had shown her foolishness by asking Rachel to do the
lodge.

'Why don't I do the lodge anyway? That way you
won't miss seeing Min,' Rachel said when Nona had
explained. Damn, damn, against you Miss Upton,
against you unless you up your bid.

Overdressed in her going-out clothes, lipstick, suit
and coral brooch Nona walked steadily down the trunk

road to Min's room. Walking steadily but vividly imagining another pace, the rush along that clean corridor if something had happened, if Min . . . It was quite impossible, it was getting worse: she couldn't think of illness these days, only death, death because she wanted it, a dead Min. Only death, as if she were going towards it each time she turned off the trunk road and approached Min's room; going towards it, wanting it but unprepared for it, meeting it unexpectedly in the clasp, the clutch it would be, the clutch of the thin white dying hand.

'How are you, my dear?' She clasped the little hand on the coverlet. Min looked confused. 'You're thinking I'm afternoon but I'm morning today. I'm going into town, dear. I've only popped in briefly. I promised to relieve Rachel in the lodge.' She tried hard to smile at Min naturally. It was hard to smile at all; the clasp seemed to be reflexive, Min wouldn't let go, like rigor mortis setting in. 'I thought there might be something I could do, get for you, some little thing, in town? How are you?' she asked, once more getting no response. She got shot of the hand and set about the bed. 'Dear, dear,' – even in illness Min managed to make everything look a mess – 'you have had a wriggly night. This quilt's the limit, Min. Let me tug it from the bottom.' She tugged and felt Min squirm beneath the sheets. 'That's much better!' Nona's hands were shaking, she fussed nervously at the fringed ends of the scarf neck of her suit – the coral brooch held it securely, ideal for Ireland . . . and the blue scarf lay partly opened in its tissue paper on the bedside table. Min turned her head to face the wall. Nona smoothed the tissue paper, a little wrinkly sound in the silence of the room.

Nona drew breath to speak and let it go again. Min would never wear the scarf.

90

If she would only say it, seventeen years; what does it mean to spend seventeen years in a convent on an island off Ireland? Explain or justify, say she was trying to reach something or avoid something – anything as long as it was worthwhile. An entry in the visitors book, a name on a list in a bureau drawer. 'You've had a good life.' Good has no meaning; Nona struggled in a situation beyond cliché. Without husband or children, in the absence of replies to any letters. To die like this made life absurd.

'No more arbitrary than an orthodox family, Julia,' but it was: no common blood ran through their veins. Julia's husband seemed like a rock in the context of Min's dying. When Nona died he'd be there and Julia and the grandchildren and a wreath from the BBC.

One was meant to use one's talents, surely? God knows Nona had drained hers. To bury your talents in a cupboard full of cleaning cloths, to drown them in a zinc bucket of soapy water . . . To celebrate your loss of personality, to strap it in, confine it, suffocate it until you became 'someone I knew vaguely'. 'Have you seen my handbag?' Not a person after all, a familiar chair, a favourite cup. Was this what became of you if you let things slide, failed to keep in touch, or perm your hair? Death's sting?

'Shrug it off like a cold, Mother.'

But she won't cry and I can't comfort her or make sense of the seventeen years. I can't make sense where there isn't any; to die like this makes life absurd. And Min is passing me the stone by turning her head to the wall, already I can feel it beneath the scarf collar of my one good suit. It's against you, Miss Upton, this reality; death was a rumour up till now.

'Someone I knew vaguely.'

'A friend of mother's.'

She wouldn't look at her, she couldn't, so frightened was she of seeing triumph in those eyes.

To die in hospital – that was the right thing, the thing for Nona to hold on to. To die like Nona's husband died, properly. Not more than two to a bed and visiting limited: protection for all the parties sadly but soberly involved. The patient was easily tired. 'Did you have a good night?' Put the grapes in the bowl, dig out a vase for the flowers, time only to ask the right questions like where to turn the water off, where was the canker powder and would it be sensible to take Sammy to the vet? A pat on the head and a kiss on the cheek and 'I've brought your clean pyjamas', a word with the ward sister if she wasn't too busy and then out through those rubber doors like a shot . . .

'No sign of Jim doing this window,' Nona said.

They were talking in the kitchen. Eileen made a pot of tea.

'Min's got a hospital visit after lunch. The ambulance car's coming across for her.'

'You're planning to go in, aren't you?' Rachel said.

'I was.'

'The town's empty—' Eileen began but Rachel interrupted her.

'If you're going in you can go in the ambulance car with Min. That way we kill two birds with one stone.'

Oh God, thought Nona, be fair. Come on!

'No one needs to suffer pain these days,' Rachel continued. 'She doesn't mind going in. She knows it's for her own good.'

'Thank God for the ambulance car, anyway,' Eileen said, taking the tea bags out of the pot with hardened fingers. 'Le Directeur took her all the way in last time. Jeez, I thought I'd die! He never took a driving test at all that boyo, worse than Jim – in any other place than this they'd banned him long ago.'

We're friends, Min – leave me alone now, won't you? Don't drag me down with you. I only wanted to go into town to get away.

'That car of his is awful. He drives like a maniac on any bit of straight. I thought I'd faint. I mean, with someone ill you feel it for them, don't you?'

'Only an overnight bag, Min,' Rachel said, packing it. 'You'll be back before you know it. Nona's travelling with you all the way.'

Jim waited outside in the corridor while they got her dressed. He was the odd-job man and the trouble with secrets was that nobody knew. 'The woman you are dressing I've undressed.' How ludicrous that would sound. Age was a costume you couldn't take off; only in drink were there any possibilities. But when Rachel beckoned him he put a good face on it, his knees creaking as he lifted her from the bed. 'All right now?' hating the lightness of his load. 'Back tomorrow, is it?' She was breathless, of course, but the eyes still had it. 'You're radiant, so you are, Margaret,' he whispered in her ear.

The effort of dressing had exhausted her. Everyone talked at once.

'Watch yourself with that ambulance driver now!'

'All right now?'

Jim carried Min out to the car.

'Some style,' Eileen said.

'Bye bye, Min.'

'Be good.'

'God bless you.'

'Is Miss Upton quite comfortable there in the back?'

'Bye bye.'

'That's right.'

'Take care now.'

What a nice pram.

'It wouldn't be a surprise to me if they kept her in,' Eileen said when the car had gone a decent distance from the door. 'Take her to Galway, Dublin even.'

'Oh, I don't think they'd do that, Eileen.' Sister Basil looked distracted; last evening le Directeur had brought her a letter. The letter at last.

'Pity I hadn't the van for visiting like,' Jim said.

'All we can do is pray,' said Sister Basil, thinking of the letter. 'Did you say to Miss Upton to light a candle, Eileen?'

'I did, Sister.'

'They'll keep her in now,' Eileen said to Jim. 'She'll not be coming back here now.'

'Nonsense,' said Rachel, tidying people up and getting them off the drive. Richard was already in the garden, and with more rain forecast he wouldn't stay there long.

'I'm going to get some nice wool for a bed jacket, Min.'

This wasn't worth the effort of reply.

'There's Iggy waving to you from the gate.'

I'm not blind, Nona.

'You'll crick your neck if you do that, Min. Min dear, do turn round, don't stare. Are you uncomfortable? Do you want to stop the car? I'm sure it won't matter if we're a little late. Shall I ask him to open a window? Open the big one and close this little

one? I'll close this little one, shall I?' Nona said, closing
it.

'Fug,' said Min.

'What dear?'

They crossed the wet strand slowly, the telegraph
poles marking the road.

'I thought I might be glad of my mac,' Nona said.
'The sky looks black over Cleggan.' As they moved
on to the tarmac road the family of dogs set up a loud
barking, with Prince ahead of them, chasing at the
wheels. 'I hate it when they run like this. I always
think one of them is going to go under the car.'

'They're wise to it,' said the driver, veering sharply
round the corner, past Reihill's, past the church, past
the phone box that Min had stood in, and pondered
in, and never, never used.

'Julia's quite right about washing woollens. You can
put them into the machine but they're never really
soft. Even with fabric conditioner. A wool mix, something with acrylic in it does make sense, you get
the . . .' When Jim had his van he raced through those
dogs and it was on the hill approaching Carneys' that
he'd lost the clutch. Min used to watch him go, sometimes crossed over with him and walked back. Was it
the spring or autumn of that year that they'd found
the house? You couldn't be unhappy by the sea,
somehow you just couldn't. For a little while she knew
she had what other people long for. Even then the
wind had made her breathless and she never learnt to
take it slowly in her stride. Pace, that's what the nuns
had tried to teach her, pace. Wind; she rather liked it
and she let it beat her up. After a while you could tell
from the sky where the weather was coming from – tell
if you cared to find out. That afternoon she had
dawdled and got caught. She'd taken her shoes and

stockings off to walk across the strand; she liked the feel of the ridges under her bare toes and the fresh wind against her legs. She'd been into Reihill's and bought a bar of chocolate; that was freedom, surely? The weight of the chocolate in the pocket of her dress. The shopping she'd done in England; the crates of tonic water, chicken breasts, dog food, dry cleaning. Chocolate in her pocket and the usual struggle to put back shoes and stockings when your feet are wet. The trick was to walk on the grass for a bit and dry yourself off. The fields were full of boulders then, as now; that was Ireland and Ireland didn't change. The boulders were like the Church: you could step round some of them but they were always there. And Iniscara still had more wild flowers than you could find almost anywhere: sea kale and sea campions, thrift and mayweed, orchids, sea lavender and trailing pink sea bindweed.

The wind blew her dress out like a balloon one minute and hard against her calves the next and when the rain came it was cold and exciting, not at all gloomy, the earth smelt as if on cue. Standing still you could see, literally see it coming at you, from over the headland beyond the promontory of Ross's Point. She sheltered in the rank of broken houses along the edge of the sand road. That was the first time she sat in the corner of the last house; their house, the house of Margaret and Jim. You felt no age in there, with no furniture, no doors, no windows and no roof, crouched in the corner of the gable end it was simple just to be. Here they shared the secrets of 'God Bless Mother' that Jim had scratched on to the piano lid in the house at Auchrisbeg. Of Margaret prematurely born on the teardrop of India that used to be called Ceylon. The end of the family, the Benjamin, the Min. Min the fiction they created, always small but very stubborn, wife of Robert, mother of nothing.

Sitting in the ambulance with my best friend, out for a ride in the pram. On my own again beneath the covers, worried over, taken out and weighed. 'You're my house,' she'd said and distinctly it replied, 'I'm anybody's.'

XXI

Jim sat on Min's bed with his tool bag and thought about mending her window.

'You're not the man for it the day Jim.' He talked to himself as Nona touched herself; too long living on their own.

Last night he thought of how he'd cross to Reihill's or go into town, chat up the Germans, try to sell his house. This morning the awfulness of reality left him sitting on Min's bed.

It wasn't that he hadn't loved her, or didn't still, it was just . . .

He was not cut out for her, that was all, not the man for the job. Sure it was sweet to remember the beginning, remember putting the flowers in the house for her, meeting her there. He'd had the van and the bike then; the bike was nearly as fast as the van.

Sure he remembered, one night now, the times he

was sleeping at Carneys' barn. And coming back and crossing over in the dark, mad so I was. Collecting flowers all the way for her and in the darkness most of it was grass; and how he'd got their house decked out. It was a nice touch, that. No jar to stick them in and sticking them in the darkness into the gaps between the stones. It took some doing but though it might look like a child had done it, it was the work of a man. Hopes and dreams. 'You don't have to see a future in it,' she'd told him; 'there's no future in anything much.' He didn't like it when she talked like that. 'All of us, any day, could be run over by a bus.'

A bus?

Metaphorically.

Metaphorically was a problem though he didn't say it out. Maybe it could have worked and maybe it couldn't. Not right for her, the house in Auchrisbeg; you couldn't go on shutting up conversations just with love. So he stayed a bachelor, but he didn't forget her. It wasn't that he hadn't loved her or didn't still, it was just . . .

Here, like, on home ground with the whole world watching you, with Reihill, his uncle and the aunt. Without money he couldn't even take her to an hotel.

'We don't need money,' she said. 'If all the waves were money I wouldn't try to catch them.'

Metaphorically.

Perhaps she knew she had it then; did she? That she wouldn't last it out. That winter, work took him away from her to England; and I never forgot your birthday Margaret, even if I did get someone else to do the fancy writing in the cards. Could it have been different, could it? And one day it had struck him, like the tide all of a sudden running out. He was old. The bungalow accident buggered him before his time and now here

99

he was like the old men he remembered from his childhood; uncles, cousins, coming into the small houses sitting it out by someone else's fire. Rolling a cigarette, taking a wee taste of crayfish, joining in the talk. A winter building, a summer on the boats.

He wasn't cut out for it, he came from a different tribe, but it wasn't that he hadn't loved her, didn't still.

XXII

Min came back, light flickered, routine as comfy as a shoe.

Sister Ignatius Antony was helping Sister Agnes to 'dress' one of the little wooden bracket wall shrines on the trunk road. Two lilies balanced nicely in the glass vase, three lilies toppled the vase which fell – God was with them – on to the blue velvet cushion on the polished floor beneath it where later they would place that special book, open the illuminated page on the feast of the Immaculate Heart of Mary and, wise to the rushing wind, hold the page in place, discreetly, with a handful of needlework pins.

Sister Ignatius Antony helping Sister Agnes: a small courtesy in the definition of the roles. Sister Agnes was too old and too disabled to do anything but suggest, and suggest she did with vigour and conviction: three lilies were always used in this vase for this shrine, three lilies it must be. That afternoon the vase that had always worked and the lilies that had always fitted didn't. Sister Ignatius Antony wrestled with the lilies, Sister Agnes wrestled with her patience; Sister Agnes knew that three lilies worked, Sister Ignatius Antony knew that two lilies worked, that three lilies toppled the vase and that Sister Agnes wanted a third lily in. Both wore grey aprons and grey sleeve-protectors for the task, although the lilies held no speck of dust and the glass vase held no water. In and out the lilies went, silk flowers fraying at the edges – the same three tall flowers, carefully preserved from feast day to feast day, epitomising the essential conflict of convent life: that nothing but the best was good enough, that nothing that could still be used could ever be thrown away.

When the lilies toppled for the fifth time both sent up a silent prayer. Sister Agnes remembered the days when all the niches had been dressed like this for feast days, the days when the *Sacred Heart* hung in the kitchen, the days when she'd held the position of Novice Mistress and Sister Ignatius Antony had been a young girl in her care. In her old age she was actually becoming less conservative rather than more so; the little freedoms of Vatican II delighted her and although she was unaccustomed to making even a trifling decision on her own she felt no nostalgia for the old days when the simple fact that something had always been done in a certain way was quite sufficient for it to continue thus, even when there ceased to be any reason for it. Inishcara at this time of year was a carpet of wild flowers and, seeing the younger sister near to tears, she suggested that perhaps this year, for once, Our Lady might prefer some wild white flowers instead. She watched Sister Ignatius Antony striding away from her down the trunk road and saw her own failure as Novice

Mistress to teach her to walk decorously, hands clasped, rather than swinging at her sides.

Nona heard their voices but didn't feel like joining in.

'Buck up, Mother.'

'I can't, Julia, I can't.'

Suffering always happens when someone else is opening a window, or something like that – Nona couldn't remember the full quote. Tears of disappointment welled behind her spectacles.

'Really, Mother!'

Something in your eye, Julia, something under your nail. Being made to feel a fool – it's always the little things that hurt.

Nona's package was light but awkward to carry. She placed it carefully against the wall and then leant against the wall for a moment herself, fishing a handkerchief from her sleeve.

'Have a big blow. That's better.'

Wherever Richard was, he wasn't where he said he would be. Probably got absorbed in something, forgotten, called away perhaps – not his fault. Well, now she had the afternoon to fill. Again. Better take the package back upstairs; she wasn't leaving it in the kitchen. She felt self-conscious about going into the kitchen at all these days: it seemed that only she had time to talk. Wearily she picked the package up once more and walked down the trunk road on the way to the back stairs. From somewhere came the sound of banging, Jim working or the wind perhaps; recently the convent had seemed so desolate to her, so quiet. In other years she'd been busy – that was all it was and not being occupied was embarrassing; she wasn't used to it, that's all.

Sister Ignatius Antony rushed past her with a jug of

water and a bunch of flowers. She couldn't bring herself to ask where Richard was. Round the corner she met Sister Agnes, standing in her walking frame.

'What have you there, Miss Upton?'

The old would talk to the old.

'Now at last a pair of steady hands and calm nerves. Miss Upton saves the day for us, you'll see. Miss Upton has brought a cloche from town for the new garden,' she continued, turning to Sister Ignatius Antony. 'You might take it outside for her and leave it in the shed. Miss Upton can arrange a few flowers for Our Lady, no?'

Probably. Nona stuck the flowers into a ball of soaked Oasis which was crumbling at the edges. Once more she felt dangerously close to tears.

'Our Lady is reducing us all to tears this afternoon,' Sister Agnes said. 'For us it is hard to change from our old ways. I was thinking about the days when all the niches of the saints were dressed, but work, work. Life was not meant to be easy, eh? A dull day today again and the garden is only for the young in this weather, no?'

Nona escaped to start her knitting. 'Commit yourself, Julia, it's the only way.'

The ambulance had dropped her on the edge of town and she'd walked up and with Min behind her she'd had a lovely afternoon. She knew people in the shops and they knew her – 'Greetings and nods from all sides, Julia'. Jim had touched his cap to her as she was crossing the street, and they'd met again later on and he'd spent five minutes asking her, had she got her messages, where was she off to now – all that. She'd felt confident and happy, joked with the girl in the shoe shop – 'Feet are like teeth, Miss Upton' – and it had been easy in such a buoyant mood to nip into the ironmonger's and buy a cloche. Her heels clicked on the polished floor; she closed the door of the Salle carefully – another door that banged, walked across to the bay windows and looked out. There were boats on the water this afternoon, families on holiday. She twisted the wedding ring on her finger; it felt tight, a ripple of fear ran through her.

She would start her knitting straight away, but she felt shattered, suddenly quite used up, as she settled herself with needles, wool and pattern in the wing-backed chair. This room was really a lot cosier at night when curtains closed off the enormous seascape, red turf in the grate, electric light and conversations over cards. Electric light made it look smaller; in the day-time, at this time in the afternoon, the ill-assorted furniture failed to fill the room.

'Come on, Mother, the others left hours ago.'

'What?'

'Were you left on your own, Granny? On purpose or by mistake?'

She put her glasses on to read the pattern. Start with the back – it was always a bugger. Cast on 111 stitches. She would do the ribbing and a dozen rows, with a pattern as loose and quick as this one she'd be up to the armholes in no time. The ribbing and a dozen rows and if Richard hadn't popped his head round the door by then she would go out and find him for herself. Knit two, purl two.

'Mother only goes there because she insists she has a role to play. For the first time in her life she has a decent part . . .'

Slip wool forward over stitch, slip back stitch over.

'The last time she went she came back moaning because she'd been recast.'

*

The woman Richard knew her to be – sensible, cheerful, urbane – put on a little lipstick, changed into her outdoor shoes, her scarf and short cord coat and went out into the gardens to find him. It was as well to remember, she thought, that of the two of them his life was probably a good deal bleaker than hers. He had never married, his mother had doted on him and gone off with a Frenchman, he tended someone else's garden, he collected inkwells. Damn! She could have asked Eileen for some coffee to take down. It was her fault entirely, her mood, the upset about Min and not his slight, for goodness' sake, forgetting one appointment! It's about time your granny did a bit of growing up.

But when she got down through the garden, for he wasn't by *The Bliss*, he was nowhere to be seen. Oh well. She'd have a good walk round now she was dressed for it; she'd inspect the maze and then she could talk to him about it, show an interest. Not a lot to take an interest in; it seemed all right to her, a bit weedy in places on the outside. Then she walked the inside of it. Min had always been silly about it since a dream of children stuck in it. They'd have to be pretty hopeless children, Nona'd said: the hedge was never more than four feet high. She wondered as she walked what it was that Richard did to it: clip it, brush its little cinder paths? It wasn't as if a roaring public broke bits off it, stuffed it with crisp papers and Coke cans. Sheep were a problem though; he had trouble with marauding sheep. She remembered the spring when sheep had beheaded every one of his tulips by the lodge. Perhaps she could help by raking the cinders a bit; she wouldn't dare to clip it, had no inclination to weed it, but raking could do no harm. Fearful that he would turn up whilst she was away, she puffed back up the garden to the potting shed. She would rake the maze and then erect the cloche in the knot garden as a surprise.

Jim was in the shed reading a paper – it gave her quite a start.

'Could I take the rake for one moment?' There were piles of newspapers in the shed: it was Jim's task to tie them up, the nuns gave them for the blind or something. Jim was eating; he didn't seem to hear her.

'I'm disturbing your tea?'

'Not at all. Come on in. How's the knitting?'

'Oh, coming on very well.' Nice of him to ask. She should have spent more time with Jim; this trip it was as if she'd seen him properly for the first time. How nice to have a normal, pleasant reaction to something, simple not complicated. 'Actually I've had to stop. I'm almost up to the armholes.'

'A fast knitter.'

'I believe I am.'

She stood with the rake, chatting. He'd made it quite cosy inside the shed; it was much colder down by the maze. At least he'd have a conversation with you – more than you could say for some. But, oh dear, a pathetic specimen really; drank, obviously – the fluttering hands.

'We missed you at the piano last night.'

It was his turn to look pleased. 'Will you take a bit of the flask?' he asked her.

'Well—'

'Tea.'

She wiped the rim of the plastic cup with her hankie. He cleared a space for her on the bench.

What a lot of stuff. The nuns collected everything collectable: bottles, bottle tops, bundles of newspapers, boxes of tins that Jim was expected to weight and sink. Yes. And she'd seen one of those plastic-covered wreaths floating at Booters Bay when she'd crossed in the ambulance car, hoped Min hadn't seen it – the graveyard was fast subsiding into the sea.

'So what do you get up to, Jim, when you're not over here?'

'I've the house.'

'Oh yes, of course.'

'Maintain it, like.'

'Yes?'

'It's a responsibility.'

'I'm sure it is.'

'The roof, like.'

'Quite.'

'Have you a house in England?'

'A flat actually, a small flat, rented.'

'Handier than buying, is it?'

'I'm afraid I didn't have much choice.' He looked rather disappointed by her lack of property. 'My daughter has a house.'

'You've a daughter. How old?'

'Oh grown up, in her thirties. I'm well over fifty, you know.' Why not come out with it, if just to him, and it was impossible to guess how old he was – worse than the nuns.

'Over fifty?' He seemed genuinely surprised.

'I'm well preserved, if that's what you mean.' She smiled at him, he smiled back. When he smiled he had a really nice face. It was cosy in the shed, unexpected, intimate. 'You never married?'

'I did not.'

'Perhaps the right woman never came along.'

'Ah now.'

They sat quietly together. She thought perhaps that he was a bit simple or perhaps that she'd just grown too used to the beastliness of London, not used to what was simple or straightforward. The tea was laced with something, too.

'Well, if you're surprised at my age I'm surprised you never married,' she said warmly. 'I believe in marriage.'

He nodded.

'Life's difficult without a partner. My husband died, you see. A long time ago, of course. I sometimes wonder, though of course I'm very used to being on my own after all this time, wonder, what life would be like if he had lived? You know what I mean, don't you – all the ifs and buts.'

'You have your daughter.' She looked doubtful. 'Doesn't she live near you then in England?'

'Oh yes, she does, a couple of stops on the bus, that's all. It's just that' – he was charming – 'you know?'

He didn't.

'Well. Put it this way' – she struggled to explain – 'In England we don't really go in for families, not big families like you do over here. You see? And sometimes I think that, well . . . I don't really like her very much.'

'Is that so!' He laughed; it seemed a laughing matter, she laughed too.

'What an awful thing to say!'

'It's the whisky talking!'

'In that case I think I'd better stop!'

'Ah, come on.'

'Well, I shouldn't really. All right, one more tiny sip. Drinking in the afternoon – what will become of me?' She sighed. If she'd known him better, if he was someone else, she might have told him anything, everything. 'The first two drinks stimulate, the third depresses,' she told him, remembering a phrase of her husband's.

'Really?'

'Well, so they say. You have one – I'll stop while the going's good.' He looked offended by her refusal. 'We all absolutely love it when you play,' she said. 'It must be a natural talent?'

'I'd lessons.'

'Really?'

'Mrs Reihill taught me.'

'Really. How interesting. I didn't know she played.'

'Used to, like.'

'Of course. So you've always lived here?'

'On and off.'

He sounded a bit maudlin. 'We hope you're going to play tonight,' she said cheerily.

'I might have to pop across.' Yes, she thought, for a drink.

'Well, another time then,' and when he failed to reply she moved to get up.

'Miss Upton?'

'Yes?'

Oh dear, he did look terribly unhappy, close to tears. 'I have enjoyed our little chat,' she said; and then he put his hand out to her and ridiculously she took it – how embarrassing!

'Will I leave the rake out for you?'

'No, don't bother. Too cold for me to be raking at my age.'

'The thought that counts, then,' he said.

Nona went to Benediction. She thought Sister Basil

looked very gloomy and said as much to Eileen. But action works, she thought later, tucking into bread and butter. Put your faith in action and it always works. You can't depend on other people, unless you're ill, of course, like Min.

'I've had such a rich afternoon,' Rachel told her.

'Have you really, dear? How nice.'

'Richard and I just talked and talked. It amazes me how one man can hold so much knowledge in his head.'

'Books, I imagine.'

'I think having a wide grasp of things is terribly important.'

'Yes.'

'We've been discussing philosophy.'

'You've covered the Elizabethans, then?'

'Pardon?'

And after supper she went with Rachel to visit Min. Min was sleeping; since her trip to the hospital she was always sleeping. 'I'm sure it's too strong for her,' Nona whispered, 'the new medicine.'

'She's so weak, None.'

'Yes, but it's making her weaker. Where are the pills anyway?' Nona looked around the room.

'She has an injection.'

'An injection?'

'To make her sleep.'

They closed the door. 'No one told me about the injection,' Nona said.

She sat up knitting long after Richard had gone to bed.

'I've brought some cocoa, None. I'll put it on this little table, shall I? Better drink it whilst it's hot.'

Nona knitted, scarcely looking up.

'You mustn't upset yourself, None. I think she really wants to go, you know.'

'Do you?'

'Subdue shock by anticipating it. That's what the nuns say.'

'Really?'

'What astonishes me, Julia, is how a man like Richard can find anything interesting in a girl like that.'

'It's obvious, Mum.'

'Not to me it isn't.'

'Because she is a girl, she's young.'

'Yes, but Richard's so, well, cultured, so English . . .'

'That's what men are like, Mum.'

'Not Richard.'

'All of them.'

'Like what Julia? Tell me what men are like – I don't think I know. Your father wasn't at all like that.'

'He didn't have the time to be.'

'You're very hard, Julia.'

'I'm right.'

XXIII

Jim ordered some flowers for Margaret and got the money to pay for them from Eileen. He had time for a wander in town next afternoon whilst the girl at the florist fixed them up for him. He was just thinking how he would have change for a drink and some chips after he'd paid for them, sorting out the change in his trouser pocket, when he felt the hand slap him on the back.

'Coming in for one?' It was Doyle.

'I am not.'

'Come on.'

'I've no money.'

'Sure I'll get you one.'

Jim deliberated, fingering his change.

'What's that you're after jingling?'

Jesus wept! Wasn't he jingling the coins in his trousers as they stood there? He would give Doyle a quid or two and be done with it and have a little one himself.

They were drinking with some Germans in the late afternoon. Doyle was carrying on as he always did with the drink on him; 'Up that like a rat up a drain,' he said of some wee girl. Jim watched television in the sad way that drunks do, an arm across the bar. Doyle was going on somewhere else.

'I'll not bother the day like,' Jim said.

He bought a drink for an English fellow in the Irish army now married to a local girl and living in Recess. Doyle seemed no sooner gone than he was back again: he'd money from somewhere, anyway, enough for a couple more drinks. Jim slipped off to the gents when the wee girl from the flower shop came looking for him. A big bouquet, it was enough for a wedding and a funeral. The German bought it eventually, though by then someone had made a hole in the cellophane with a cigarette.

How sad the heads of the foxgloves looked, bowed down by the rain. It did not occur to him to pick them; he walked back from the town empty-handed and alone. He'd picked her a bunch from the hedges before now but he was younger then and he'd never felt older than he did now.

He would tell her what he'd had a mind to tell her this long time. The cellophane bouquet might have embarrassed her perhaps. He'd wake her anyway, call in on her and make her a present of himself, for Mother of God this night he has precious little else. His trouser pockets were empty, the legs wet round the ankles where he'd missed his path. He went in by the kitchen, stepping as quietly as he could in the sleeping house. He went in to her, held her hand for ages, so it seemed, before she noticed him at all. He felt the tears coming then and he didn't bother stopping them; it was nice like that, the two of them quiet in the dark.

Later he rolled a cigarette, opened the window. She was weak perhaps, she didn't need to talk; he did.

He did the talking then: told her how the wind was getting up outside as he'd crossed over. Her face looked like a monkey's in the moonlight, it was that thin. Her hands felt cold so he pushed the basket chair nearer to the bed and held her hand in his hand under the cover. 'Warmer now,' he told her and when he squeezed her hand she squeezed back. He wondered, did she remember the time he drowned the kittens? He told her how their souls were somehow still in the bucket when he'd walked back from the water. Not for long, like, but long enough so that you'd know it. He believed in the soul, he said. God's merciful, he told her, and she'd no need to worry on that score. And if she went he wouldn't be long following, for he'd his fill of all of it, and specially the likes of Mr Doyle. They'd had good times and it was his fault that it didn't come to much. Both of them were fit for more than crumbs under the table, if not in this world then the next. And, starting to cry again, he told her not about the flowers the German bought but about that time way back. When he'd stuck the flowers in the old house and how the sheep had eaten most of them by the time the two of them got back. He should never have gone to England; he'd missed her there as much as he did the sea. God would have made us perfect if he didn't want us to make the odd mistake. England was one of them, and in any case it was the sinners, the imperfect ones, that Jesus said God most loved. And there had to be something anyway with everything created so particular the way it was; and night and day's the same for you now, Margaret, as, in the drinking bouts, it's often been for me. Our souls are immortal and dying middle-aged had more to say for it than hanging on and getting old. Margaret would not thank God for the life of Mary Reihill, would she, for the arthritis and the bitterness of his mother's sister in Moyard? When she'd gone he'd probably go back up north with Sylvester. The convent was on the way out anyway, but whatever happened he'd not be away for long. I've a feeling I'll be joining you and that'll be the time for the two of us in heaven and some crack.

His monologue had been punctuated by squeezes which stopped now. He thought she was off again but when he went to close the window he could see her eyes were open in the dark. He smiled at her; she made a tiny movement with her head.

'Will I leave it open?' He came close to her, great eyes with that same stubborn look. 'It's getting wild out there, darling.' He described it to her as she lay there: 'Not many stars, windy and about to rain'. Understanding what she wanted, with great carefulness he sat her up in bed. 'You can't see it now, Margaret, because it's dark anyway.'

She wanted to stay sitting up so he took the quilt off altogether and wound it twice round her shoulders and across the bird-like thinness of her back.

'You'll be fine like that,' he told her, 'warm.'

When she was asleep again he left her but like the kittens, for a long time before he finally slept, he felt the occasional pressure on his hand.

XXIV

All day the bedding lay outside. Richard and Nona guarded it in the way that things turn out; a drying wind between the showers and, raising their eyes periodically to the windows of the Salle, they were able to move fast before each downpour, hurry together through the little garden door, rescuing the mattresses. Richard had caught a chill from somewhere, complained of a 'scratchy' throat, the long hours of morning and afternoon were punctuated by his feeble little cough.

At first Nona thought that it was sweat. She had woken early and the morning through her window had that washed-out look after a night of violent rain. She found Min sopping, breathing heavily through her mouth, the room in disarray; and remembered that all night she'd heard, or thought she'd heard, the noise of something loose somewhere, a window slamming to again and again and again. Min's window was broken: glass both on the blankets and the floor. Her face was warm and red; breathing like a horse, noisy in the calm of the island morning. Everything that Nona might have covered her with was damp; the hand towel – Nona took it from its rail and then put it back again, ridiculously small. Min breathed noisily, half sitting, half spread-eagled on the bed, the nightdress sticking to her and rucked up with the quilt, her long grey hair straggling on the pillow, one hand between her legs.

'I can't cope with this one, Min.'

Sister Euphrasia was on her way down the trunk road. Nona resisted the temptation to run at her. They approached each other deliberately, the baton of responsibility passed from hand to hand.

Rachel took away the sheets and blankets, Eileen mopped the floor.

'Careful now, Eileen,' said Sister Euphrasia as they handed each other the bits of broken glass. Jim and Sister Ignatius Antony set a precedent, between them they got the bed into the corridor. A mattress was brought from downstairs. Nona made the bed up, Rachel dressed Min in a fresh nightie; she was tucked into the bed in the corridor with clean cellular blankets and a hideous crocheted quilt. Inside the lay-by Jim taped cardboard cut earlier in the kitchen across the window-frame and so whilst he worked at it Min lay in state outside, snoring in the middle of the trunk road, flanked by the niches of the saints, altering the traffic flow; but whether she regained consciousness and enjoyed the heaven of being where she was, or simply, in her coma, thought she was in heaven, no one ever knew.

The doctor, ferried across the high tide by one of the young Dorises, told them it would be over in a jiff.

Nona helped Richard with the mattresses; would be over, would be over. Try as she might to empty her mind, she failed to rid herself of the snoring, spread-eagled indecent Min and throughout the day had no other vision of her old friend.

'You're so fortunate, Nona,' Min had said so many times. 'You've done something in the world, you are someone, all the letters you get, those interesting people . . .'

They turned the mattresses. The doctor dithered and agreed to stay for lunch. Eileen was behind-hand in the kitchen, Rachel sat in the porteress's lodge and the nuns fussed over the doctor as they did with any man.

What a long morning, a long jiff.

They had rosary in the chapel and Sister Euphrasia sat with Nona afterwards, encouraging her to knit on with the bedjacket for the missions, exclaiming in wooden English how much fine work she had already accomplished on the back.

The afternoon became unusually warm, quite summery. It seemed inappropriate to go out in it but the battle for the mattresses was won. So they all sat, the largest gathering for a long time, grouped together in the bay window of the Salle. Rachel with her rosary; Sister Ignatius Antony, a Girl Guide of a nun today, a pal and chum; Sister Euphrasia, spurred by the knitting to talk about the Congo, her mission to the piccaninnies in 1951. Sister Basil prayed, Sister Agnes stared out of the window, Sister Godeleive, eyes closed beneath dark eyebrows, a film star mouth. Rachel with her rosary sat amongst the sisters and at no point during the afternoon did she allow her back to touch the chair. Nona knitted and at the card table Richard reversed the order of his hand in a game of patience. The door banged but it was only Jim, his long legs making it to the bay window in no time, apologising and saying 'No, just the same'; a telephone rang and was answered on the fifth bell – probably for the doctor, Sister Basil said.

'She had a good life.'

'Out of her misery.'

'Blessed release.'

'We are all terminally ill,' Rachel said at lunchtime. Richard shivered. 'Death's the only certainty,' she said.

The sisters came and went on unexplained errands, communicating with each other by the movement of a finger or the plucking of a sleeve. Jim followed Sister Agnes's long stare out of the bay windows and saw himself sitting in this room and in other rooms – plenty of practice sitting; over at the Dorises' helping one of the younger boys by threading up his line; across with the Reihills for his Sunday tea, the polyester tablecloth with the Celtic interlacing, the round tower, the Connemara ponies, the harp and the cross . . . That day when he first saw her, it happened in a clap. No one knew; it was hard to believe it, like a sky rocket over the island. Headlines for him. No right words to describe it; he couldn't believe it didn't show. Stirred him like a spoon. Walking it back from Carneys', the necks of the foxgloves in the rain . . .

Sister Euphrasia left the circle, closing the window Sister Ignatius Antony had opened, and not a word was said. No ticking from the digital clock but the rosary clicked the time away. Richard cleaned out his nose with a hankie. The tea bell when it came at last surprised them all. Well fed, the doctor left shortly after tea; and shortly after that Min died.

XXV

Nona sat with her elbow on the corner of the kitchen dresser, quite still as if posed for a photograph, ready to smile. She would sit like this for taping an interview, her elbow on the corner, the mike in her hand, but she wouldn't tape an interview in this kitchen; she was drinking a cup of coffee there. The ceiling was high and the floor uncarpeted; the acoustics for taping were bad.

At the table Sister Euphrasia was cutting up vegetables, soft to the knife as if the muscle and spring had gone out of them. Eileen was baking; when she opened the oven a blast of hot air flushed the faces in the kitchen. Nona watched. Requiem mass at eleven; Min's body had come back, the lay-by reverted to a parlour. The kitchen furniture, including the chopping table, was ranged against the walls, lined up in this large room as if about to be shot. There was a gap in the middle which meant that Sister Euphrasia had to cross the floor again and again to put her peelings in the hen bucket. It irritated Nona to watch it; she thought of Julia clicking her pedal bin with an accustomed foot.

The two women worked together in silence, the radio, out of decency, turned off. Silence; Nona couldn't tell if it was companionable or not. Eileen picked – a piece of carrot, a corner of pastry – licked her fingers and wiped them on her skirt. Nona tried to think about the mass. Min was the gap in the middle of the kitchen; she might be the explanation of its silence or she might not. Rachel had told her that Min's soul was in purgatory, that in purgatory you expiated every sin that you'd ever committed, that Min had been specially lucky to die in a convent. Specially lucky old Min. She'd chosen some odd meal-time readings the last few days, all 'Stir up thy soul, O Lord': Rachel leading St Dymphna's into the last battle – the drama of Min's soul in purgatory seemed to have gone straight to her head.

'And there are nuns, you know, who don't believe in purgatory any more.'

'I believe in it,' Nona said.

'Emotions are so complex, aren't they, None, but God is there for all of us: "Seek and ye shall find."'

He wasn't in the kitchen, that's for sure: a blank gap and space. The soup would be left to simmer all through the burial and the mass. She wanted to shout at Sister Euphrasia to get her by the throat: 'Don't you know anything about food? You should speak to my daughter about cooking vegetables. Lightly steam, you idiot, never boil!'

Rachel was already in chapel, wearing a headscarf, kneeling up.

Not much of a send-off, Min.

No sign of your sister-in-law or your husband. Me, Richard – whose cough has turned into a mouth ulcer, quieter but equally irritating – Eileen, Joe Reihill and Jim there at the back. Cahill Doris looks too small to carry more than a suitcase. That's seven on our side and six on theirs, including Monsieur le Directeur. Thirteen. Eileen, using her sister's missal scrawled with pop songs – 'Saturday Night Fever', 'Stand by your Man' – made it fifteen including Min and God.

'Look at the suit on him,' she whispered to Nona. 'Dad, not Jim.' She smelt of sweat after the baking, her nails were full of flour. Suffering always happens when the nails of the person next to you are full of flour. Perhaps it's just that suffering always happens?

Monsieur le Directeur taking his time about it, in bad form, according to Eileen, over some trouble with his parishioners about saying an Irish mass. Three men and a boy carrying your coffin, treading carefully down the slope; Richard, stuffed with Rinstead pastilles, by far the best dressed; Cahill Doris no better than his brother.

'Would you credit carrying a coffin in those shoes?' Eileen whispers to Nona as they leave the convent gates. 'Thank God for the tides anyway, just imagine if we'd been cut off. I'm after reading a terrifying account in one of Rachel's books. There's this woman and her husband went over to some tiny bit of an island off the Blaskets, where they had some sheep, Tuaisceart it was I think, and he was taken bad. The weather was terrible and they couldn't get off the place or send a signal or anything. He died on her and then she couldn't get him to the mainland or get a message, and he was that big a man she couldn't even get him out of the house! The weather never improved for weeks and the island kept cut off – and you've no idea what that poor crazed woman did, Nona! She cut him up, in pieces – she was that desperate to get him buried. When they found her she was a near maniac sitting up in this old hovel with bits of blood and flesh all round her. I've a theory that's why we've our own burying place here.'

Richard prayed hard: I know you despise dishonesty, so thank you God, for taking Min this time and forgive me for such a base emotion. For some time I have not been confident – the tide of blood in my calves, the pain I get behind my ear and the tingling in my fingers. I did sit with her once a day since July and any suspicions I had about her character I kept to myself. And I would have confessed them but I prefer to go direct. I have also come to the graveside despite a chill that threatened a temperature – I don't mind doing that. I must ask you this morning, being honest, how much credit exactly have I got? If you could show me in some way, give me an idea how long, a rough estimate obviously. I'm sure I'm not the only one here this morning thinking of myself – not really me but Rachel and the lettuces. If there was a tithe I would gladly pay it. You keep us all so much in the dark. I should be used to it by now but could you, this time, tell me? I see you in the inkwells, you know, oh yes. I can't handle them often but each time I take them out I think of you. Of you creating craftsmen . . .'

'It's as well she's the last one, with this graveyard slipping,' said Eileen. 'Dad says there was a wreath washed up in all the muck at Booters Bay. They say the EEC is coming down here to assess for compensation. Sylvester sent his wishes but he had to mind the shop . . .'

XXVI

Min's death affected the community like a green light, like watching the end of a train.

Eileen and Sylvester had been down to the convent at Shannarara to demonstrate an inflatable castle in a little playground he was setting up: a small investment, hours of fun – the west coast had never seen the like. Jim was going down there later to make a start on the adventure playground; Sylvester had ideas for a death slide. For the first time in a long time no one looked for St Feichin's footsteps, meant to appear in the sand at this time every year.

'Times are changing' Sylvester said when Nona mentioned it in the shop. Even the Aran islands had suffered this year, he told her: one woman had said to him that it was like visiting India when you got there – all that begging on the quayside and nothing exciting to see. No islands were out now on account of the bad state of the weather and the boats: people needed more than sea and scenery and a bag of chips. Only academics and geneologists went anywhere out of the way and they were tight with the little money they had. And on the state of the graveyard Sylvester said that Inishcara itself could slip into the sea for any great difference it would make. Times were changing and not before time.

Eileen agreed with him, or she said she did. Sylvester had the knack of including everyone in his expansive plans; he had a way with him, could charm the leg off a stool. She was fed up with the kitchen anyway, so she said. Sylvester had treated her at Shannarara; she came back in plastic earrings, matching hair combs and a large slide in the shape of a bow. She said she'd had enough of cooking for people who didn't appreciate her food, that she'd never used pepper in anything and wasn't starting now. To be honest, and she was usually honest with Nona, the place was getting to her: she couldn't stand a death.

'Look at it this way,' she said to Nona, 'Maureen's life's set now, isn't it, and mine could be anything I make it, so Sylvester says. All Maureen did was find a husband. I'm more ambitious than she was, and in any case I'm plain.'

'You look very pretty when you're dressed up, Eileen. You've got a lovely smile.'

'Smiling into this sink for the rest of my days – no thank you! I'm glad the convent's closing; it can't end soon enough for me.'

Even Rachel, who had worn Ireland like a grass skirt, had had enough of it. These days she sported a smashing cap and gown. 'It isn't just financial, Nona: the Church is a living, changing body, don't you see?'

She was awfully up on recent church history – Taizé, the ecumenical movement; she spoke of institutional adaptability and organisational change. The directive from St Dymphna's mother house not merely a change of location, more a revolution in attitude; the community, as it stood on Inishcara, was an anachronism, an insult to Vatican II.

'But the service they provide . . .'

'To a tiny élite, None.'

Elitism of any sort was frowned upon. Nona saw herself drowning as the lifeboats filled up with prostitutes and heroin addicts. She had become a leper at a most inappropriate time. Grab a syringe and join us but don't keep tinkling that bell; quick, to the boats, the island's closing – hurry please, it's time.

Everything comes to an end; embrace change, give it a smacking great kiss. End: the word like the name of a lover that she couldn't stop herself bringing into every conversation; and each time she said it, 'end', they met it with the word 'beginning'. Rachel sometimes added that Nona's trouble lay in the fact that she was so obviously tired, but it was not only energy Nona needed to face the word 'beginning', it was faith.

Nona tidied out her chambrette: with a besom brush she did out the corners, with a duster she wiped over the handles of the small melamine chest of drawers. She swept under the bed, she lined her shoes up, she took a damp cloth to the window-sill and newspaper to the window panes, she dusted the top of her hanging cupboard by standing on the chair, she cleaned her basin and heard in the silence the water draining through the plug-hole and down the pipes; all this took precisely a quarter of an hour.

Sister Euphrasia had left some knitting for her in

the Salle. She ran her finger along the banister of the back stairs; beeswax and turpentine, rubbed in and rubbed off – it was dustless. Sister Euphrasia had found a tartan plastic knitting bag from somewhere, a long zipped bag: tidy, tidy, it was tidier like that. The handle of the bag required mending. Jim had not been seen for days but after some looking she found what she needed in his shed.

Things to do: find Sister Euphrasia and thank her for the knitting bag, knit. Sit down, stand up, go for a little walk? God was in the chapel at the end of the trunk road and always keen for a chat. Monsieur le Directeur had suffered two punctures in twenty-four hours; everyone was talking about it. The move meant a lot of paperwork for him, telephone calls and meetings with Sister Basil – both he and the car were under stress. An article in the local paper had condemned him for his refusal, or inability, to say an all-Irish mass. He looked gloomy even in his splendid vestments and showed no interest in Sister Basil's photographs of Gheel, town centre, satellite stations, mother house. Rachel grasped this opportunity to talk to him about the modern nuns' exposure to more profane environments and whether, considering the element of individual decision-making, nuns could choose whether to work with the ill, the elderly or the adolescent distressed? Sister Ignatius Antony commented that it was the personal decision-making that would most upset the older nuns; this would be all that was new to them, for nuns, traditionally, were fearless, courageous and brave.

'A queer sort of bravery,' Eileen said, in the privacy of her kitchen, 'not minding if you're mugged or killed in the street. You see, it's not the same for them because they don't mind about their bodies, only their souls.' Her ears were red and swollen now but silver hooks were pricey, she said, taking the earrings out now and again and putting them back with a lick. The holes had been pierced once already when she was quite small, but these were new holes as nowadays everyone had it done three or four times at least. Eileen said that there were some nice pin heels she had her eye on and that she wouldn't mind working at Shannarara. From there you could get a twice-weekly bus into town.

Rachel wrote home:

Dear Mum, apologies for the delay. I've not been able to write of late, owing to my commitments over here, owing to a death here which has really affected our little community. You remember I wrote to you about Nona, a bit of a posho but all right underneath. She's been up to high doh recently and I've had my work cut out. Her friend Margaret (known here as Min) died last week. Naturally we're all upset but Nona is the one really cut up about it and although I have yet to experience the death of someone close to me I am doing what I can. I feel so sorry for her: she looks so darn pathetic these days, wandering about so lost. This apart, everything is fine with me. The Irish weather gets me down a bit which brings me to what this letter is really all about. If I remember rightly I mentioned Richard in my last to you. We're getting along fine and I suppose it's a case of like meets like. He's a good deal older than me and brighter too! He collects inkwells and is a man of remarkable culture and faith. Well. He wants to found a community, Mum, a retreat house over in England where the weather is better and you get a different class of person all round. He wants me to join him as Guest Warden when he gets the place set up! Being a keen gardener he thinks he'll call it 'Eden House'. You can't be much closer to God than in a garden can you? I mean unless you're in a church. This community is moving to Belgium in the autumn and much as I love the sisters here I don't go a bomb on that. According to Richard it's the pits of Europe (Belgium): they're all fat and, well, you know, Mum, how I feel about that! On this point I'm eating well and good fresh food when I can. Our logo is going to be a knot garden, Elizabethan – Elizabeth I that is. I'm getting on so well here but I think I'm just about ready for another move. Must sign off now, love to Dad, your own Raitch.

XXVII

Grin and bear it. For some time after Julia and her husband returned from their weekend's assertiveness course at a hotel in Potters Bar they continued to practise not to smile. Smiling, said Julia, was both a habit and an apology. One shouldn't smile unless one meant to; smiling was dishonesty if it contradicted what was going on inside.

Nona was dishonest; lied through her back teeth in the days following Min's death. Her heart shook but she parted her lips and smiled, toned-up the muscles in her cheeks. She smiled at Abraham and at the two angels in the refectory in the picture called *The Weighing of the Souls*. She smiled when Monsieur le Directeur asked to see the visitors book for his records; she smiled when the Cluedo game went on and on and grinned when it was established that it was she, inadvertently, who had put two rooms and one weapon into the murder envelope and so confused everybody else. She smiled at Rachel's guitar, and at the card table, she smiled at the closed piano, she smiled at the copper table, the turf basket and the chairs; the old elephant forgets the ancient trackways through the forest and, finding himself cornered in a clearing, smiles. She bought a nice postcard of Connemara ponies for her grandchildren and for Andrew a view of the lobster ponds at Auchrisbeg. 'Gourmet eating,' she wrote on this one. 'Have you tried dillisk?'

She'd like to have a word with Richard but she was frightened of approaching him, frightened of the cold shoulder: 'I'm rather busy, Nona. Now what exactly do you want?' Just a little chat. 'I'm not sure what I'm doing yet, next year you know. I wondered, if you, you and Rachel, had made any plans? All things come to an end of course, I realise that. Ghastly for Min isn't it, I mean facing those overdecorated bungalows for the remainder of her days. Richard, hang on a minute, don't go. Remember that present I gave you? Well, I was torn between that and something else . . . All those funny games of Racing Demon – I mean, it can't all just end. What am I going to do? Please. Help me.' No she couldn't approach him. She couldn't trust herself. 'Tell me that you care, Richard.' No. Smile at Richard and keep smiling, knit. 'How's your cold, Richard? I think you ought to do something about that cough. At our age . . . Ha, ha, ha . . . Her feet kept leading her to find him: it was like some awful game. One evening she had turned on her heel when she heard the sound of voices outside by *The Bliss*. He and Rachel sat there now, 'a sensible place for a quiet chat, the last of the sun, out of the wind', an inspection of the knot garden. 'Did I tell you she looks just like my old nanny?'

Sister Basil looked serious, Sister Ignatius Antony looked confident, Eileen seemed upset. Eileen didn't smile at anyone except Sylvester, who expected it. Her everyday tasks had taken on a different meaning now she knew that it was ending. She saved the brave face for Sylvester; she felt sad. Chicks had died that summer; oily wings are signs of maturity and these were victims of the rain. One evening, going out to shut the hens, she saw the strangest sight. She hadn't been able to put her hand on the big torch and suspected Jim of taking it. The small torch had a loose connection and in the little light it offered it was hard to work out what she saw. The peg had slipped from the wooden hatch in the hen house and had fallen, clunk, and broken the neck of one of the brown hens who now hung, suspended, feet right off the ramp.

'God, look at that,' she whispered. She took the hen out by its feet and searched about to find something else to hold the hatch up but the other hens, finding their entrance blocked, had gone elsewhere to roost and it was a devil of a job finding anything with the torch. In the dark she traipsed round with an empty scoop – 'Chook chook, woodie, woodie' – and tracked them down eventually, perching on the private parts and roosting by *The Bliss*. At this point the torch packed up and she carried the dead hen, walking in the darkness, saying an act of contrition over her waste and her deception and hurled the body out into the sea. She doubted if the Shannarara nuns had hens, or, even if they did, in a big place like that, whether she would be in charge.

It was too dark to see Min's grave except in the beams of the lighthouse. Min was lucky because she'd died in a convent; her future was settled, Eileen's was not. What if Sylvester couldn't find her a job – what then? Was it wrong to have ambitions? Her father seemed to think it was. He said Sylvester was all mouth and plagued his very nerves.

'I am the light,' God said to her.

'Sure I know you are,' she said.

'I'll look out for you,' he comforted. 'Never worry about the hen.'

XXVIII

The hens broke the cloche and Nona cut her fingers picking up the pieces. That was that. She hung about *The Bliss* for a little while but Richard didn't come.

'You don't care if I get broken,' she said, to no one in particular. How serene the Madonna looked, stuck there in the wall, serene and stupid; what had she to look so smug about, what had she witnessed, overheard?

'You'll soon be left behind, my girl.' Like Min, abandoned, left to the long-tailed sheep. No one to clean you like Min did, religiously, the long-handled brush scooping the sand from the folds of your gown.

Cleaning; surely all that cleaning, the cupboards, the brushes, meals, prayers, visitors, couldn't just end?

So the days of August ran right out: 25th, 26th, 28th, 29th. Sister Ignatius Antony mended the hen house: an excuse to be out in the air.

And Richard felt a little better: not marvellous,

mind you, but better. He still kept tabs on his condition; he didn't want to ask again but still he waited for a sign. He and Rachel had gone through the pamphlets, done the brochures, conscientiously studied the form. They knew they had made not only the right decision but the only decision there was. He did feel better: his cough had gone, his ulcer, which had reached a crisis on the morning of the funeral, throbbed no more and when Nona smiled at him, he smiled back. Rachel had faith and zeal; he felt young in her company, virtually secure. A young girl from a young country with a mature faith; he had experience behind him, she had zest and zing. He could already see his inkwells displayed to advantage in glass-fronted cabinets, in the new drawing room . . . the new study, the new hall, the new kitchen, the new greenhouse, the new life, DV. Glorious celibacy, spiritual togetherness, almost like finding mother again. Their knot garden, a public and a private symbol of how they had groped together in the gloom of wet and windy Inishcara and how with God's assistance they had seen the light. He was the best of the old, she was the energy of the new; she would need guidance, he would need constancy. The winter lettuces at last a reality, God approached, God glorified through organic gardening. Rachel sunbathing with her top off somewhere west of Hastings, gardening gloves hanging together in the shed. She would care for him in his old age and, as founder of a retreat house, he would go straight to heaven. His experience of suffering had not been wasted. Sussex seemed to be the place for Eden House: familiar and near enough to London, super, fertile soil. Sitting by *The Bliss* in the last few days of August; so much to discuss and plan.

*

'Yet a little time is the light with you.' Nona woke with a start, the knitting in her lap, woke from dreams of rushing in the corridors and cases in the hall. In one nightmare she'd woken to find her fingers intact despite the sense, indeed the feeling, of hours of scrabbling at Min's grave. She could see the grave from the landing window.

'Mother's coming with us next year. I want everyone to behave nicely and –'

'God Mum!'

'Then we won't be able to climb up Scorry Ridge –'

'Or go caving!'

'We won't be able to do anything with her!'

'Oliver!'

'Or go on cycle rides!'

'We'll have to compromise, that's all.'

She dreamt of sand in a square room, she dreamt of sand blown in, she dreamt she had buried Min's handbag in a grave. Sister Ignatius Antony told her that she ought to have the handbag when she went through and cleared the little room. One knitting bag, one handbag; and the handbag was an excuse, wasn't it, Min? There was nothing special in it after all. I always thought you had something special in there: wads of notes. How you hated losing it . . . My handbag is full of addresses and credit cards, yours held almost nothing at all: a purse, a hankie, a lipstick, an emery board. I wish I didn't know, hadn't looked. And then, I suppose I thought you might have kept my letters – vanity again. Deep breath, fill the lungs, face everything at once; Richard probably rips up my postcards without reading them . . .

'She was always worried about losing her handbag,' Nona told Sister Euphrasia, who patiently held a skein of wool for Nona to unwind, 'and there was nothing in it to speak of.'

'Miss Warner is now beyond such things.'

She was, yes.

In many ways all of us have lost our handbags, thought Nona. Could Sister Euphrasia grasp a thing like that? Had she experienced it, that moment of sheer panic, the beginning of the end?

'Lost my bag' – it was Min's catchphrase, what she would be remembered by: 'I can't find my bag'. She wouldn't have been noticed if she hadn't lost it so often, if everyone knew what Nona knew: that it was virtually empty, of no significance, no account. But why then was she so frantic always to have it safely in her sights? The 'sorrys', 'could you move', 'excuse me', 'dreadfully silly of me', 'I'm being a bore but have you seen . . .'

She made a conscious decision to talk to Richard – she reneged. She sat alone.

'Having a lovely time. Wish you were here.'

She felt cold. Her bottom was cold. Out of the sunshine into the wind.

'Shark fishing tomorrow, v. excited.'

Something was scratched on the stone of the seat of *The Bliss*. She tried to make it out: JVA? The sheep are coming, Fanta cans, crisp packets, birds. Everything must end, Biggest Ever End. Brought from somewhere and placed here. First the long-handled brush, then the little wisp for the folds of the skirt and the face of the baby. The little wisp lived in the wooden cutlery box lined with baize. The cutlery box lived in the cupboard . . .

'Have you seen my glasses?' she would say. 'I thought I left them . . . so silly of me.'

'I saw something scratched on the stone seat; I was

unable to read it without my glasses and I looked up at *The Bliss* and . . .'

'Excuse me, excuse me but have you seen . . .?'

'Excuse me Richard, Rachel, so sorry to barge in, but have you seen . . . I seem to have mislaid my . . .'

'Eileen, have you seen Miss Upton's glasses?'

'I put them down somewhere.'

'Pray to St Antony.'

'She rushed in like a rocket from out there. She was into me in the kitchen. She said she'd lost her glasses. Trembling like a leaf she was, like she'd seen a ghost – the state of her! Always a very neat and tidy person. I never knew her to lose anything before. She always wore her glasses round her neck. Miss Warner was the one for losing things. Miss Upton wore her glasses on that cord thing round her neck.'

'I never saw her without her glasses.'

'Part of her.'

'She was holding things in, of course.'

'Bound to be a reaction sooner or later.'

'We found them in the knitting bag. Then it was you, Eileen, wasn't it, went out eventually and brought the old girl in?'

'I told her myself in this kitchen, Miss Warner – the hen, there's always a third thing.'

'I had no idea she was upset.'

'I took her upstairs and put her to bed. She looked really worn out to me. Eileen made up some chocolate and I took it up to her. The weather can change here so quickly and she'd been out a long time.'

'No one noticed she was missing – that was the strangest thing.'

'I was helping Richard to get things sorted out, you see. There was no one in the Salle that evening – so much to do with him going away, so much to do, so little time.'

XXIX

Reihill was restless in the shop; restless and, as he told
Sylvester, in two minds. Barely twenty-four hours had
passed, but he felt that the days when he'd risen to the
sound of the bread being delivered and slept again
over the counter reading yesterday's English papers
were gone forever. He couldn't settle to anything that
morning, couldn't settle down. Alternately he stood
outside his shop, looking across at the island that was
so familiar, looking at that lump of nothing all his life,
and then back and forth to the left and to the right
along the road. He'd a scene with Eileen already and
she had gone off shouting into her own room.

'You're not keeping me here like a prisoner!'

'I'll decide what to do, Eileen!'

But what to do? It was nearly the end of the season,
a bad one. Diversify, Sylvester suggested, if a bar and
a shop and a post office wasn't diversification someone

had better tell him quick what was. And a holiday house and tickets for the fishing trips and bookings for the Galway bus.

'All reliant on the thing,' Sylvester said. 'Visitors!' What you needed was something else that didn't depend . . .

He came inside again, fiddled with the closed sign, toyed with the idea of turning it round again: 'Sorry, we're closed'. And what difference would that make? They knew he was there and they'd see the car. If anyone wanted anything they came in through the bar or round the back. He took a pack of cigarettes from the shelf and opened them at once. It was a moral dilemma he was facing; he put his finger on the phrase and felt, for a moment or two, relieved.

A miracle was better than a craft shop; show him the man that tried denying that! The hired cold cabinet, the insurance; charging people for back papers and putting a penny or two on here and there, putting a whack on deliveries – the money was small and the expense got bigger every year. She said, she claimed; and after all hadn't it happened many times before? And when something like that happens what happens next? Controversy, that's what, and the media and people, people who need to be sustained by cigarettes and chocolates and coffees and drinks, crowds of people, coach loads.

She said the statue moved, she told Eileen. And Eileen thought she saw it quiver. He hadn't been there; how was he supposed to know if it did move or it didn't? He could see himself now; 'father of Eileen'. Always a good quiet girl, religious. He thought of her snivelling and threatening him from the corner of the stairs, the red ears, the wide face; an odd choice for a visitation. Lived with us all her life and we never knew she would be chosen; one in the eye for Monsieur le Directeur. He thought of her bedroom, the tape recorder, the make-up, clothes all over the floor, the posters of showbands. They'd rowed for years over the noise, the mess and the ruining of the wallpaper. Wrecking her ears and destroying the wallpaper – it was hard to decide which was worse.

She could go and destroy someone else's wallpaper, he told her, only she was a good girl and she earned good money and his wife liked having one of her daughters still at home.

He went into the bar to have one. The till glinted: 'father of Eileen?' His toy, and why shouldn't he have a toy? Mother of God, he'd worked hard all his life and for what? There was another side to it, of course: young Irish girl influenced by older English woman, head turned with nonsense; but then, looking at Eileen, you knew she was sensible and, 'father of Eileen', he wouldn't want to make her out a fool. He'd an awful headache already, he smoked furiously, his hands shook. He went out again, outside the shop, without any idea what he was looking for; in again he shouted up the stairs through the music.

'Eileen, Eileen!'

She appeared, huge and ugly, his own daughter. 'Come on down here, Eileen, till I talk to you.'

'I told you.'

'And turn that racket off! Now, Eileen?'

'The English woman comes into me looking for her glasses. Later on I found her sitting out there when I went to shut the hens. The Australian girl took her upstairs and I made her a hot drink. She says she has something to tell me and that I'm not to tell anyone else –'

'The exact words, Eileen.'

'She said she saw it move.'

'Move?'

'She was sitting out there and someone had scratched something on the stone seat, and she was trying to make it out and thinking that the convent would be empty and all sorts of vandalisation, and she was looking up –'

'In supplication like?'

'How would I know that?'

'Well?'

'She looked up and saw it move.'

'How, Eileen?'

'The eyes opened and looked right at her.'

'Eileen, you don't believe that!'

Eileen shrugged.

'What happened next? Was there anything else she said?'

Eileen shook her head.

'Did you see anything?'

'I don't know!'

'Well, think, Eileen.'

Eileen appeared to think. 'It seemed different.'

'Things would seem different, if you looked and looked.'

'It looked –' she tried to copy the look with her red face.

'Miserable like?'

'More –'

'Anxious? Worried?'

'Worried sick!'

'It's a stone, Eileen.'

'I know, I know. I know it's a stone. It's awful!' It was awful, she felt awful. 'What'll we do, Da?' she said.

He had a headache, he said, he felt awful.

'Don't let's do anything, Da?'

He gave her a look.

'Och Da, you wouldn't! She has me sworn to secrecy.'

'You told Sylvester.'

'He got it out of me!' Now Eileen started to cry.

Joe stared out of the window; the rain obscured the island and he was glad of it.

'Is she all right, this woman – not mad or anything?'

'I don't know.'

'Who else knows?'

'No one, no one, I swear it! You should have let me go across, Da – they'll think something strange.'

'Sure there any number of excuses.'

'What if Monsieur le Directeur finds out, Da?'

'Well, he won't find out. If no one tells him. And don't mention it to your mother, Eileen.'

'I will not . . . I knew something like this would happen,' she added, almost defiantly. 'Things always happen in threes.'

'Meaning what, Eileen?'

'Miss Warner's death and the hen.'

'What hen's this?'

'Nothing.'

'Examine your conscience, Eileen.'

'Haven't I been doing just that, every moment since she told me?' she shouted back at him, running up the stairs.

'I'm surprised you can think at all with that racket going on,' he said.

Was this God's way of paying for the new till? Doesn't God himself move in mysterious ways? What harm if he did tell someone? Sure, there was bound to be a fuss for a while but nothing went on and on. But it might go on. Inishcara might become a holy place like Knock. Did God mean this to happen? There was nothing much else happening, that's for sure. And Reihill's bar and grocery there at the forefront of it all . . .

'Eileen! Eileen!'

'What?'

'Come on down.'

'Da!'

'Come down! I want you to go across.'

'Da!'

'Go back as if nothing's happened but keep your eyes peeled, like.'

Eileen thought about it. 'I don't trust you not to tell anyone.'

'Don't trust your own father, Eileen?'

'I do not.'

'As sure as I stand here.'

'What if it's true, Da? What if I see something? I don't want to, Da, and I'm worried about people getting it out of me, like . . .'

'Pray for strength.'

'That's good, coming from you.'

'Go on.'

'You believe it, don't you, Da?'

'I don't know, Eileen, I don't know.'

Diversify. It had everything: boots and galvanised buckets, Ratak and fishing tackle and Persil Automatic and matches and the cold cabinet and papers, disposable nappies, shampoo, cement. Everything anyone wanted within reason – but not enough people to serve. This place had nothing, not even weather, and all the old dears coming in for two wee slices of boiled ham and a corner of Galtee cheese and dog food and stamps for America. Craft was where the money was and, according to Sylvester, playgrounds. Was God about to give him something, like the Arabs got the oil? And how he'd overcharged the convent all these years . . .

'Eileen! Eileen! Get down those stairs till I speak to you. Eileen!'

He went out the back thanking God Sylvester had seen fit to go to Shannarara after all. He got himself a cardboard box and dashed around the shelves, filling it with groceries with shaking hands. Would she ever carry that? His eyes ran to the boxes of Ratak and the tower of tinned tomatoes, bent cans that hadn't moved. He forced himself towards the corned beef and pink salmon. His mind ran to a set of spice jars but he put two packets of Nutall's Mintoes in instead, 'thinking of the weight you see . . .'

'What'll I tell them?'

'Say nothing.'

'But . . .'

'Say. Jesus, I don't know! Say I struck it lucky.'

'Oh no, Da, please!'

'Say. Say your mother sent it – they'll swallow that. Say I've nothing to do with it at all. Go on, for dear's sake, Eileen!'

Coaches instead of kittens round the bins, a full bar, a queue at the shop, the computerised till working it all out. He stood outside watching his daughter as she crossed, balancing the cardboard box on the handlebars of her bike. 'I'm just saying what she told me; I take no responsibility. I'm only passing on information fed to me by her, like a computer like, you know. I'm not saying that as a family we're more religious than the next one; it's a matter of being in the right place at the right time. Who am I, Joe Reihill, to question the goodness of the Lord?'

XXX

The sunset was gross. Like an airbrushed painting, a technicolor sci-fi, drug-induced epic. The windows of the Salle provided a frame for it. The digital clock read 20.51.

'I just can't believe this is happening to me,' said Rachel.

It wasn't. The deep colour spread out all over the sea. In its vulgar light Rachel's face looked tanned and wholesome; Nona's teeth looked yellow and her face quite grey.

'Happening to little me,' said little me. 'It's the most exciting thing that happened in my life.'

'Perhaps that's why you were saved from death.'

'Do you really think so, None?'

Red sky at night and tomorrow would be fine – fine a bit too late. The farmers' crops were already spoiled; everything was spoiled now; and at the end of the trunk road, outside the bathroom still called 'Office', the phone rang.

'That b. phone!' Rachel said, quite worked-up.

Nona listened to the phone. It had been ringing all day but orders had come not to answer it now.

'Just who do they think they are? Ringing a convent so late in the evening. I never saw Sister Basil look so riled.'

Nona looked at the sunset on the water, thought how tomorrow would be fine. Oddly it was her legs that felt tired this evening, as if she'd been standing all day. The weather had been really summery: a little breeze off the sea, no rain, she wished vaguely for open-toed sandals.

'I still can't really take it in,' continued Rachel.

Shut up. Shut up.

'I offered to pay. I think Sister Basil's really rotten not to let me ring home. I mean, if they didn't have the money from us guests they wouldn't be able to afford a phone.'

It would be dawn in Australia, would it; the beginning of a spring day? Could they skip a day here and go into night so that tomorrow didn't come? The setting sun would rise again. Nona wished for a Red Sea of her own devising that would close off the island for good, but the weather was set fair: no tidal wave, no gale-force wind, no act of God could save her from tomorrow. Believe it, believe it, believe you me.

'Though now I come to think of it,' Rachel said, 'Sister Basil's reaction is not really so peculiar. You can't be too hard on them, you know. I mean, people react so differently to crises, don't they? I suppose I'm just fortunate in that I've always had it in me to rise above such things. Rise to the occasion, you know, take things in my stride. God made us all different. I

148

normally find that the world can throw anything up at me these days now that I have HIM. It sustains me somehow, keeps me calm. Richard, you know None – he really was upset! He really didn't want to go, None; he felt awful about it really. A real struggle for him, you know, God he was upset. But once you've made arrangements – I mean in England it's almost Bank Holiday. I mean, if you're a friend you want to act like a friend. It wasn't his fault having to go off. Well, I'll say it again, None, Richard may not be able to be here but I'm your friend, you know that.'

Not a lot to say to that one. Nona was so tired, she was past it, too tired to answer or to arrange her face properly; her mouth sagged.

'I am selfish going on like this. You're tired None, too tired to think straight I don't doubt.'

Julia and Rachel both knew what was for the best.

'I want you to go to bed, None.'

'So that you can answer the phone?'

'No. No one's going to answer the phone.' The mild voice.

'Why don't you take it off the hook then?'

'I will if you want me to.'

'I can't stand it ringing.'

'It's stopped now, None.'

Nona got up. In her head the phone kept ringing. The lozenge cloth covered the piano; she played with its tassels, lifted it off a fraction, lifted the lid of the piano and struck a chord in the silence. And then, as if on cue, the phone began again and Rachel got up too and stood beside her.

'Why don't we go somewhere where we can't hear it?' she suggested, because she didn't have the guts to take it off the hook. Sister Basil had told Rachel that she didn't want to see her near that phone. 'Why don't we go and make ourselves a nice milky drink, eh? Then we could go to chapel for a while?'

'No.'

'Oh come on, None. Perk up. Here you are, chosen for something quite amazing,' her voice was an intimate, reverent whisper, 'and you don't even want to go to chapel?'

'No.'

'Come on, None.'

'I don't believe in God.'

'None!' Convulsively Rachel clapped her hands over her ears; then her hands were holding Nona's hands on top of the piano.

Nona laughed.

'You're getting hysterical, None.' Rachel's voice was really serious. 'I think it's time to calm right down, don't you? I tell you, I wish Richard was here now.'

They stood in the middle of the room holding hands over the piano. 'He always protected himself,' Nona said. 'It's his secret, like his inkwells; not keen on direct light.'

The kitchen was neat and tidy despite the earlier lack of Eileen.

He always was a bastard, Nona thought.

Rachel warmed some milk. 'I won't sleep tonight, Nona,' but Nona kept her distance, placing her hands on the clean cold tiles and holding them up to her face.

'They'll want to talk to everyone you know, interview us all.'

'That won't take long.'

They'll want to talk to everyone . . . but where is everyone, thought Nona? You had to hand it to him really; God's script was rather good. Here I am stuck with Rachel, no Eileen, no Min, no Richard, no Jim.

They went up the back stairs together. The phone

was silent now; maybe the exchange had simply given up. Sister Basil had spent much of the day ensconced in the porteress's lodge with Monsieur le Directeur. Nona had taken those early calls but after that Sister Euphrasia had come down with a message for her to stop. Sister Basil had been scrupulously polite: 'We can manage in here for today,' she said, when Nona presented herself at the lodge; and Nona had taken her last look at Abraham and thought then of the Red Sea. Her privileges had been suspended; no tone of voice, no special look, no strait jacket, but Nona knew and Sister Basil, Sister Euphrasia, Sister Agnes, Sister Godeleive, and Sister Ignatius Antony knew she knew: her services in the lodge, not today thank you or ever, any more.

Her chambrette was immaculately tidy. She washed her hands in the little basin to get rid of the feel of Rachel's hands. She opened her window and looked out. Turning away from the window she sat on her bed and looked around the room. The sponge bag, her beauty sleep cream, hairbrush, blank postcards held in an elastic band, biro pens and a tube called 'Dinner Party Pick-Up' – a face mask that she'd never used. She must go to the bathroom; she picked up her sponge bag – how tiring it all was. She sat down on the bed again and looked at the sponge bag closely as if searching for a clue. The eye make-up remover pads – an extravagance for holidays, freshen-up pads, cotton-wool buds, flannel, toothpaste, her stoppered bottle of '4711'. What did those numbers stand for? She had absolutely no idea. A tube of Polos in her handbag, but with shaking fingers she couldn't get one out. The way things were packaged these days! 'Blisters from Blister Packs' – that could have been a filler, a little talk, three minutes, '4711'. Her career was finished, wasn't it? Mentally unsound. The notes, three lines. 'Three lines on anorexia.' Food: 'How the Pineapple First Came to England', 'A Day in the Life of a Penny', 'The History of the Orange', 'Making the Most out of Tropical Fruits', 'Easy Meals on a Pension', 'What's in Your Sponge Bag That Doesn't Make Sense?' Julia wouldn't get her here; the voice she'd spoken to over the phone had been Irish, American? Reihill's papers came a day late but the press would be here in person tomorrow: young men like Andrew, the sort she'd always been frightened of, the sort who wore blue, Chinese work suits instead of jackets, shirts and ties. They played with you, unnerved you; even their sexuality was ambiguous. 'There is no respect for our generation – I was having you on, Min. They don't care; experience doesn't count. I plead with them, if you really want to know, I beg.' One in four people over sixty, '4711', don't count. Vicious ambitious young men, educated young women who spend a fortune at opticians on impressive and intimidating frames: 'I'd like something a little redder, larger, squarer, more menacing.' Stuck on an island looking out to America, sitting with her sponge bag on the bed. Saturday night. Shaking my Hermesetas tablets in the tin. On Sunday mornings she and Richard liked to listen to broadcasts by Alastair Cooke. If it was day in Australia was it day in his part of America too? She wished she could ring him – Alastair, not Richard, as a colleague, one to one, for help. She left the chambrette on her way to the bathroom but found herself feeling her way down the cramped back stairs instead. In stockinged feet, sponge bag and towel over her arm, she padded around the familiar silent house. It was never really dark there: the light lasted much longer and there was always light by the winking statues and beneath the chapel door. She found herself standing by the phone; a phrase of Scott Fitzgerald's, muddled as usual but something on the lines that it was always three o'clock in the morning. Emotional bankrupts should stick together. Oh for normality! If only it was 10.15 p.m., a concert from the Queen Elizabeth Hall coming across the sea, sounding like cricket from India; listening to the radio and Richard fussing with the cards, Eileen putting the hens to bed, Min doing the rounds on her last search.

'Have you seen my glasses?' What had she done?

All five nuns were in chapel for the night litany. Sister Basil had told her once that the convent routine was so rigorously followed that the sisters could be sure that whatever was done on Iniscara was also being done in Belgium, in America, New Guinea. Such security. The sisters of St Dymphna, oblivious of time zones, singing through the small hours of the night.

She sat at the back of the chapel, her sponge bag on her lap. 'Mumbo Jumbo' Julia called it; but if there was a God would he realise that Richard was a rat? She imagined Julia's kitchen, the light, like the altar light, coming on each time she opened her well-stocked fridge. Raising her eyebrows, speaking into the receiver, mouthing the words 'For Granny' to her children and 'Hang on I'll get her for you' and 'Mum, it's Alastair Cooke'.

XXXI

The day was neither here nor there; the forecast was 'intermittent showers'. Sylvester had probably overdone it with the ice cream. Eight a.m. and a strange Volkswagen Polo parked just up from the shop. Now that irritated him – not to know how long it had been there, whether it had anything to do with 'it'. Normally now Joe might take a dander up there, make conversation, do his bit like for Bord Failte, but he didn't want to seem too eager or too foolish. He had to admit to being just a wee bit disappointed not to see at least one coach in the car park but Sylvester, who was dogging his steps this morning, told him, 'Give it time.' The tide didn't open till two or half past, Sylvester was all for taking the van across then, sweets and drinks and sandwiches and ice creams, drink, of course; but Joe was worried sick about his neighbours and particularly Monsieur le Directeur. 'If you don't get in there someone else will': but the thing about it was he had to live here, not Sylvester. Perhaps he should let Sylvester pack the van, take the van, but could he trust Sylvester not to pocket what he took? He flicked the curtain and looked at the Polo again. If only Eileen would have stood in for him at the shop; but Eileen had gone all holy on them and categorically said she would not.

The logistics of the operation were worrying. It was hard to plan ahead at eight in the morning when you had no idea at all of what the day would bring; a better man than he would find it tough. If he got someone else in he would have to pay. 'Think big,' Sylvester had said when they discussed this but Reihill was used to thinking small. Now: say he took the van and left Sylvester in the shop, he'd never cope if he got a rush on in the bar. He'd suggested Jim, though doubting he had the wit to do it, but Sylvester had him in check once again: 'You're out of touch, boy.' God in heaven – the way Sylvester went on! No. Jim was away with it altogether, spending money as if it was going out of fashion. He'd spent a night with the Gardai Monday last and was only out now because some crony of Doyle O'Riley's had seen fit to stand him bail. He was a wild man when he had drink on him and more than likely to start a fight. Sylvester had shown Joe a piece in this week's *Tribune* but Joe could hardly concentrate on all the little print.

'So there's no Jim to help today?'

'There is not.'

Out of habit Joe was now unwrapping the English papers. 'Dear God!', rubbing his chin with blackened fingers and thinking that he must take time to shave.

'I don't know how I'm fixed at all,' he grumbled.

'Is there no one else you can call on?'

155

'There is, but I'd have to pay them, boyo. Cash. What if the day proves to be a great big nothing – what then? I'm left paying out good money for two fellows sitting on their arse.'

'Think big, man.'

'I'm finding it hard to think at all.'

'You've Eileen, for one.'

'You take her and I hope you've better luck than me! No, I best shut up the shop.'

'That's ludicrous and you know it. Sure there be more takings the day than you've had all season, Joe. Go on, give someone a call.'

'How can I call anyone if nobody knows? It's not me going to be the one that breaks the news.'

'Sure they'll all know soon enough.'

'What do I say?'

Sylvester shrugged. 'In a couple of hours there won't be anyone between here and Galway who doesn't know exactly what's been going on. Common knowledge soon enough and they'll all be cashing in.'

'But how do I phrase it like?'

'Almighty Christ!'

'You do it then.'

'You're the one knows everyone. Who is it you get in when you're busy?'

'I'm not busy.' Reihill raised his fist and thumped the bundle of newspapers. 'You don't know the half of it. There's been no one busy round here for years, Sylvester. You think you know it sideways, don't you? You're here for a couple of weeks in the summer and you know it sideways. I don't need extra help – sure I can hardly make a profit paying myself.'

'You'll have to get someone in today for I'm out to the island in that van.'

'I suppose I could call the Dorises?'

'Good on you.'

'Get Enda in the bar and Cahill serving?'

'Go on.'

Joe hesitated. 'Just say there's a rumour of a moving statue on the island. Trade's going to be good – say it out like, think big, say you'll give them both ten pounds in their hand.'

'Ten pounds!'

'For minding things from after dinner like, from one on.'

'Ten pounds – you're codding me!'

'For Jesus' sake, Joe!' yelled Sylvester, losing his patience and his charm. 'We've the van' – he paced the words out slowly – 'and there'll be television cameras. You'd better believe it so ring the Dorises now!'

Very reluctantly Joe went over to the phone. Sylvester followed him round the bar.

'There's a fresh car out there,' he said.

'The Polo?'

'Another one, a BMW.'

'It's likely the Germans from down the road.'

'It's someone anyway. They're waving at me, so they are. I think we'd be in good time to open up the shop.'

'I don't open till nine,' Joe shouted after him, dialling the number.

'It's not a normal day, Joe.'

'Damn right!' said Joe, his hand over the mouthpiece of the phone and standing up to check the numberplate on the car. 'You're right, Sylvester,' he said with excitement at last lifting his voice, 'It is not!'

'The Dorises are fixed,' he told Sylvester a minute later, almost running in his slippers to open up the door. 'I'll shave and you and I will pack the van. We'll take Eileen with us.'

157

'She'll be needed at the convent?'

'Not at all!' said Joe, convincing now at last. 'You tell Eileen that I want her here where I can see her. If they're giving out food at St Dymphna's they'll not be buying it from us.'

'You're catching on slowly, boy,' Sylvester said, smiling and squeezing his older cousin's arm.

'Well, catch yourself on and get that door open,' Joe said, taking the stairs at a run, 'and check the mixers in the bar!'

XXXII

All things as they always were in the place and the country that Nona had always secretly considered to be her proper home. Red sky at night was an English myth; the Irish had their own ideas about it. She watched the last day of August dawn. Misty rain, a sky that brightened briefly over Carneys' barn where Jim was sleeping, a little early morning sun but clouds banking over Ross's Point: the air had little warmth in it and without the benefit of a weather forecast Nona anticipated rain. Richard had been right to leave; the summer, what they'd had of it, was over. A wave of misery struck Nona, who knew that she must get strength from somewhere and stood at her little chambrette window dabbing her neck and forehead with cologne.

She hadn't slept; she felt as wretched and as raped as the stretch of sand on which St Feichin trod – the

gap between Iniscara and the mainland when the
tide took the sea out beyond Moynishmore and
Muckinish on one side and Currickluhan and Feroonagh on the other, pushing the water that was left
into the muddy graveyard of abandoned boots and
shoes and cookers in Reihill's corner, Booters Bay.
Across the water she saw a tent in the Germans'
garden, two cars parked at Reihill's and what looked
like a Dormobile van.

Standing at her window in her dressing gown and
slippers she went through it like a script.

I was upset at my friend's death. I thought I saw
something – perhaps a trick of the light? I was distressed; I know that now. I told someone because –
you know, a problem shared . . . I am sorry for all the
trouble that I've caused . . .

So you believe you were mistaken?

I don't know what to believe.

You are confused?

I am an old woman (say it, say it), distressed,
demented, scrap-heap stuff.

I gather the convent is due to close, that the nuns
are moving to Belgium?

Yes.

If it is a moving statue it could be the kiss of life for
the community, couldn't it?

I don't know.

You've been coming here for a number of years,
Miss Upton?

Ten years.

So St Dymphna's means a lot to you?

It does.

So it might have persuaded you to see the statue
move, if you were in that frame of mind, so to speak.
What frame of mind were you in, Miss Upton?

Can you tell us again?

Where were you sitting?

Are you a religious woman, Miss Upton?

Have you visited Lourdes?

Your friend is buried on the island?

Do you believe in miracles, Miss Upton?

How long have you worn spectacles?

Did the statue speak at all?

Did it bleed or anything?

Do you have a special affection for St Anne?

You're a creative woman, Miss Upton. You would say you had an imagination? You say your friend Eileen was with you later that evening. Was it dark at the time?

Why did Mr Crosswhaite leave so suddenly? You said you were old friends?

You were in charge of the hospitality here on your visits? Did you enjoy that job?

This summer can't have been a good one for the convent. You enjoyed your position in the convent. Publicity was your aim. Self-publicity?

Why do you think God chose to manifest himself to you? What makes you special in his eyes?

You say you are not a religious woman, Miss Upton. You mentioned sheep. Do you consider yourself to be a lost sheep?

How do you think the nuns are taking this, Miss Upton?

You haven't discussed this with the nuns. So this is really nothing to do with them but rather between you and God? They are religious, yet he chose you?

They say God moves in mysterious ways, Miss Upton. He seems to have been particularly mysterious on this occasion . . .

Have you a message for your daughter, Miss Upton?

God!

What are your feelings on Knock, Miss Upton?

What do you think of the tradition of hospitality?

Would you describe yourself as especially devout, a religious woman?

A mad woman, an old woman, a scrap-heap woman, an hysterical woman, a lonely woman.

You are a widow but you have a daughter?

You depend on the convent?

You always come here for your holidays?

You say your friend died recently. You have no other friends?

So you would feel a little lost if the convent moved to Belgium?

A desperate woman, a silly woman.

Your Australian friend, she tells me she is opening a retreat house across the water?

A jealous woman, a contemptuous woman, old, lonely, wretched, mistaken, dishonest. Ordinary, frustrated, hardworking, committed, true—

To your career or to Catholicism?

Granny?

What are your feelings on the Irish situation, Miss Upton?

What is your position on the IRA?

Do you think visitors to Ireland have a right to be apolitical?

Do you have any other Irish connections?

This love affair: is it with Ireland or the convent? This island?

Why did Miss Warner die?

Why did Mr Crosswhaite leave?

Where is the girl Eileen?

You immersed yourself in Irish literature, in stories of the old Ireland?

They are Rachel's books.

So you are not interested in books, Miss Upton?

Not those sort of books.

Would you say that you had desecrated a holy place by making its name famous?

Mr Reihill is making an honest trade.

You are an honest woman?

Have you ever been prosecuted for shop-lifting?

Have you private means?

Do you pay the convent for its hospitality?

Where will you go? What will you do?

Your broadcasts for the World Service; could you tell us something about those?

You say the World Service doesn't count because it's for foreigners. Could you expand on this?

Would you say you didn't like foreigners? That you wouldn't have felt happy in Belgium?

You say that Ireland is not a foreign country. Is that because you consider it to be a rightful part of the United Kingdom?

You have always praised the individual in your work, Miss Upton. Was it you as an individual here, deciding to act perhaps?

You make a good salary from your work?

You are badly paid. Have any of the newspapers offered money for these interviews? Would you consider taking a payment?

Is this your way of breaking into television, Miss Upton?

You preferred a career to the religious life. You say you don't do anything for charity. Do you believe in charity? Is your daughter religious? You don't 'get on' with your daughter. She has her own ideas. You don't agree with these ideas?

Live and let live.

So you'd describe yourself as '*laissez-faire*'?

You have lived alone for a long time?

God?

You never remarried?

God?

You mentioned something about the simple life. About cards and conversation. About recognising shop assistants, about lifts in on the sky road between here and town. About knowing your path down the trunk road and not minding the chapel door closed. About the door into the garden and the purple of the maze. About always having the same bed and the same view from your window. About your home from home, Tara Iniscara . . .

God!

God!

I'm on my back in an Irish field, the razor wire cuts and the light's going and I'm feeling very weak. I am unable to contact Mr Cooke.

XXXIII

Jim wanted to be blind drunk, oblivious; he couldn't sink the pints fast enough, get enough of the right stuff down. His clothes, his breath, even his hands and his hair smelt of alcohol and yet he couldn't get enough down him, couldn't afford the whisky chasers that would do the trick. He took his drink into Mary Reihill's bedroom but soon left her. A week spent at other people's firesides was enough. Some hours later in the confusion of the public bar, Enda Doris, whose brother ought by rights to have done the serving, gave him a bottle on the slate.

And as Jim drank his bottle Nona held court in the Salle. It didn't look nearly so silly with all the chairs filled and, glancing to her right, she saw with a mixture of pain and satisfaction how thoroughly the RTE helicopter had clipped the veronica maze.

A pat of the hair, discreet clearing of the throat.

165

'You have to make it intimate, Julia, a technique, act it into the mike'. The small grey elephant took her chair.

'Thank you for coming. Are you all comfortable? Is that piano stool really all right?' And I'll play for time till I've got your faces and you will, won't you, bear with me? 'I'm afraid that I might go round the houses rather.' She dissembled more like a cat with a mouse than an elephant, and of course they would bear with her.

'Take as much time as you need, Miss Upton.' That dotty perm, the sadly shabby bag, those glasses on a cord around her neck.

And 'I'm not used to seeing my audience.' They don't understand this but they smile to reassure her and imagining the green light she says, 'Richard Crosswhaite saw *The Bliss* move.'

The pause is perfect; suspense and suspicion stir around the room. 'W-H-A-I-T-E.' The reporter nearest to her extends his microphone as she might have done. She smiles, they smile; the elephant in a clearing who has never addressed an audience before without a written script.

She must make time and take time; giant pander is the order of the afternoon. 'You're busy people, I know that: homes to go to, deadlines to meet. For once I don't envy you your job. You're here to draw the line, aren't you? To pencil in the point between miracle and hysteria, truth and fiction.' I'm only an old elephant. 'I shouldn't like to do that.

'Richard's character, his credentials? Well, I've known him for years, you see. And we've corresponded, a man of few attachments, only his mother – as Irishmen you do have the measure of that; we've grown old together in our summers here. He's a quiet man, bookish, a collector, by no means an hysteric. We didn't see quite as much of each other this summer as I should have liked; he had one or two new interests in the convent grounds, plans too (and all the worry!) for founding a new retreat house based around an organic garden – across the water somewhere.' She and the press dismissed the retreat house; 'I'm one of you,' she seemed to say – it was understood that England didn't count. 'And marriage plans too, I believe.' The audience perked up. 'Still, it was me he chose to confide in, old friends and allies, me he chose to speak to you this afternoon. And at this point I should say what I should have said at the beginning,' – more smiles, this isn't easy – 'that in a way you've arrived both too early and too late. Too late to speak to Richard personally and too early, I fear, to see the event in its true context, metaphorically and literally, too early to see it in an appropriate light. To understand fully what I know he would wish me to explain to you, you should stay with us till the last of the sun. Because you know the tide will change I expect you won't stay long enough: you'll leave before the water closes, before the sea can cut you off. This room's shabby now, no setting for a miracle, but you'll have to take my word for it, my dears, when I say it can be beautiful, really beautiful, almost heavenly.

'Here in the west the light lingers and in the summer evenings this room is transformed.' She pats the hideous director's swivel chair on which she sits. 'Beautiful, and heaven lies beyond that little door. It's the place, you see, not just the disputed stone madonna, the place we call *The Bliss*. Oh, if you could see it in that light! Richard and I have spent so many happy evenings sitting out there, in the shelter of the little wall, enjoying the last of the sun.

'As I say, I didn't see much of Richard this year. I've been coming here for ten years now' – hardy perennial – 'but this year's holiday has been quite different almost from the start. I didn't sit out by *The Bliss* much, not because of the rain – what rain we've had! – no, the stone seat there is only made for two and – marriage plans, I didn't like to interfere. Is love blind? I wonder. I'm very fond of Richard and I did not foresee his coming marriage. Richard says he saw *The Bliss* move and yet I'm ashamed to say that it was me, on my own there by the stone madonna, me who waited for a sign. If I sat there long enough I felt certain he would come to me. He did come but the miracle he described to me was not the miracle of which I longed to hear.

'I'd say faith implies a leap of the imagination, wouldn't you? The assumption of Mary, the transubstantiation, the transfiguration of Christ, Lazarus, St Joan and St Bernadette, Richard Crosswhaite and *The Bliss*. A retreatant's thoughts dwell long on just such mysteries; but where to draw the line, you ask me, what is what? Richard and I – round the houses, I did warn you – let me speak for just a moment about age.' Pause, breath, courage.

'Richard is fifty-six and I am sixty. He collects inkwells, I make broadcasts. We are ordinary people, quite unexceptional; why should God choose one of us? We are neither middle-aged nor elderly; in blunt modern parlance we are post-menopausal and pre-retirement, we inhabit the unlabelled limbo in between. There isn't a word for us that I can think of. We're able-bodied, we have emotions, but we're hardly visible: you wouldn't recognise either of us if you met us twice on the same train. I said we had emotions; we feel things, and the thing we feel most keenly, most pertinent to our meeting here this afternoon, the thing we feel most keenly is that we can't be sure. We live in hope, I think, to a larger extent than you do, and it isn't the loss of our looks but the loss of our confidence that we mourn. What do we believe at this age, what can we believe in? We aren't sure. We face our own mortality; we hug our own religion but at this age even our deaths are robbed of tragedy. The death of one of our number diminishes us perhaps more than you may understand. The deaths of close associates and friends and the shifting of the rest of it – the shock for us of the closure of this convent! – the shifting of the rest of it is hard. Our senses dim and our confidence wanes; we aren't as sure as we used to be, we dither. What have we seen, what have we imagined, can we hope? The pathways through the forest are familiar and yet we hesitate, waiting for a sign. To go back is impossible, you understand, and only death, an unremarkable private horror, lies ahead. We only know that we no longer can be certain of anything much at all; we only know from our experience that suffering always happens and we wear it like a stone around our necks.'

A sip of water, thank you, thank you. A shuffling and a coughing, a movement of reporters' buttocks numbed by poorly upholstered chairs.

'Richard says he witnessed what must be a miracle; even the elephant's instincts shudder in the face of an event like that. And I am the one he chose to confide in, to bear his burden I suppose. Marriage plans – but you see how close we still are, the old bonds; he chose to pass his little secret on to me. You're here to draw the dreaded line and I can't help you. A difficult task, one might say quite impossible, but the public do have a right to information, I've always been whole-

169

heartedly in favour of all that. All I can do this afternoon is present Richard and our communal life here
in its proper light, and I do hope there aren't any
cynics among you, any one of you who might harbour
the suspicion that what Richard saw or said he saw
was, in the context of his future plans for a retreat
house, a rather unsavoury example of advance PR.

'The evidence is inconclusive. You've been very
patient with me but I've really gone on far too long.
One thing I have learnt in sixty years is that facts can
only be cornered surreptitiously and must be treated,
should you really catch one, with caution and great
care. Feelings are much less slippery objects, loyalty is
tangible,' a twinkle with Min's eyes, 'and all I can
really say of Richard's strange confession is that I'm
proud that he chose me.'

The tide had turned again; Booters Bay was just a
stagnant puddle. Mrs Reihill flicked the curtains at
her window: most of the reporters had departed but
there was still some activity down by the beach. Dogs
barked fiercely.

'It's the Gardai, Joe,' she called out. Beyond her
line of vision an outboard whirred and choked, whirred
and choked again and finally burst into life. The
Dorises were out of their house now – 'There's something on, Joe'; another car, more barking. She saw the
Gardai talk into their car telephone and watched
fascinated at first, then later with horror, as one of the
Gardai and a German in waders hauled a body, a
body she recognised, from Booters Bay on to the
beach.

Unaware of what was happening and shouting this
and that in to his wife to keep her going, Joe Reihill

turned the calendar beside the colour television in the bar.

'It's bad luck to do it early, Da.'

'Sooner be a day ahead than a day behind,' he said, as he always did.

'There's a scene on the beach, Da.'

'Enough scenes for one day, Eileen.'

'Come on down and see what's happening.'

'You go,' he said and chewed the quote for a moment: 'The stone which the builders rejected, the same is become the head of the corner: this is the Lord's doing.'